I0531631

Inaccurate Realities
A Young Adult Speculative Fiction Magazine

Volume 5

Monsters

Inaccurate Realities: A Young Adult Speculative Fiction Magazine
www.inaccuraterealities.com
Volume Five

Editor: Christa J Seeley
Assistant Editors: Andrea Modolo, Sara Eagleson
Proofreader: Danielle Webster
Cover Art: Sara Eagleson
Social Media: Jaaron Collins
Image Credits: Canstock photos csp22310475, csp22107393

Inaccurate Realities is a quarterly magazine.
Published out of Toronto, Ontario.

Contributor guidelines for writers and artists are available on our
website or can be requested through:
submission.inaccuraterealities@gmail.com

Table of Contents

Letter From the Editor

As some of our readers may or may not know, Inaccurate Realities is based out of Toronto, Ontario (Canada). And if you've been following the news you know things haven't been great up here recently. A lone gunman stormed our Parliament buildings and killed the soldier guarding our War Memorial. And then one of the most prominent faces of the Canadian Broadcasting Corporation was fired from his position and accused of non-consensual sex acts. All of this is extremely troubling, and it has affected Canadians from coast to coast.

So it's fair to say that these recent events were weighing heavily on my mind when I sat down to write this letter for our "Monsters" issue. They made me think about how our ideas of "monsters" change as we get older. When we're younger we're scared of what might be hiding under our bed, of the ghost in the attic, of the Dalek on the television set. But as terrifying as those unknown creatures may be, they are contained. They stay in their realms and eventually we stop hiding behind the sofa.

Unfortunately, that doesn't mean the monsters are gone. Only that they've changed. As we get older we find that our new monsters are hidden in plain sight. They could be our colleagues, our neighbours, or even the voice coming through our radio. And if our early childhood monsters were enough to scare us, the knowledge that the monsters now walk *among* us should cripple us with fear.

But it doesn't.

If anything, we've seen the opposite happen across Canada recently. We've seen people stand together, speak together. We may not always agree with one another, or even see eye to eye on these particular issues, but they do affect all of us and we've shown that we aren't willing to stay silent or simply hide away.

And you can see that sense of camaraderie and community in the stories of our fifth issue. The people who stand up and fight don't do it alone, they do it together. Because ultimately standing together is the only way to keep the monsters at bay. Whether that monster be a Minotaur or a homicidal parasite or an alleged criminal, we must not forget who we are and who we want to be as a community.

So enjoy the stories and keep on supporting one another. It's what separates us from those things that go bump in the night.

Happy Reading,

Christa J Seeley
Editor
Inaccurate Realities

Labyrinth Hope

S G Larner

The girl flicked her long blond hair back, smiling into the camera. "I'm not worried," she said. "Beauty tames the savage beast, doesn't it? Do you think he could resist me?" Her sculpted eyebrows arched and she leaned forward slightly. The camera panned down to her golden cleavage. The screen showed her odds—six to one—then cut back to the host.

"Phaedra has had a surge in the last minutes, to take the lead. Our dark horse, Theseus, is at the bottom of the table, at one hundred and twenty-nine to one. In just over twenty-four hours, we open the doors to the Labyrinth!"

The screen cut to commercials.

"Why did you audition?"

The boy shrugged. "I had nothing better to do."

The two sat in the holding cell, waiting for the thick steel door to open and admit them to the enormous Labyrinth constructed beneath the Acropolis for the show. A camera mounted on the wall tracked their every move. So far twelve teenage boys and girls had entered; they were the last.

"Really?" The golden girl sounded dubious. "That's not really a reason."

Theseus looked away. He had a long dark braid down his back, hair longer than the girl's golden mane. "Mama died from cancer. Papa left. There are no jobs. As I said, I had nothing better to do." He glanced at her. "You?"

"Fame. I want to be an actress." She opened her mouth, hesitated, then shut it again. He noted the subtle make-up applied to her already-pretty features. The enhancement made her beautiful.

"If you survive," he said.

She pursed her lips.

"You do understand that you'll probably die?" he asked.

"I'm not stupid. I will stay out of its way. Anyway—" she flicked her hair back "—the producers like me."

"It's not rigged, you know," Theseus said.

"Isn't it?" She smiled at him.

He didn't like the sound of that.

Oooonnnnng. The sound of the gong echoed through their cell. They stood, faced the heavy metal door.

A voice boomed over a loudspeaker: *"And now, last but not least, Phaedra and Theseus!"*

"Oh, god, I'm so nervous," she whispered. "I want to throw up."

Theseus laughed. "It's too late to back down."

Ooooonnnng.

Theseus shook her hand as the third gong sounded. The door swung slowly outwards. "Nice to meet you, Phaedra. Are you coming?"

She froze, staring out into the dim corridor. He beckoned impatiently. She stared at his long fingers with wide, scared eyes.

He sighed and saluted her. "Stay alive, hey?"

Then he sprinted into the darkness, leaving the girl behind.

Phaedra stood before the shadowed entrance, shaking. *Move,* she thought. *Just put one foot forward and go.* Her giddy confidence had all but evaporated. *They said I'd be safe, that there were ways to get me out.* "It's going to be all right," she said. *Ugh, they will use this footage for sure. MOVE!*

She poked her head through the opening and took her first good look at the Labyrinth. The dank sewage smell turned her stomach.

There was enough low lighting to see several metres down the grey-walled corridor, after that it became a vague blur. The passageway was empty, no sign of Theseus or the other contestants—nor the Minotaur, thankfully. Phaedra inched out, head high, listening for any stray noise. The silence was broken by her footsteps on the uneven cobbled ground and her harsh breathing, but she heard nothing else.

A raw scream pierced the quiet. Phaedra faltered, coming to a halt. The scream cut off, and in the sudden silence her heartbeat thudded in her ears. She glanced up at the walls, but the cameras were well hidden.

"One down." She hugged herself. Then she gave herself a mental kick and crept deeper into the Labyrinth.

Theseus slowed, dropping back to a brisk walk. He had taken so many twists and turns that he was hopelessly lost, but he didn't care. The death scream of his fellow contestant still rang in his ears.

He concentrated on slowing his breathing and took in his surroundings. The walls this far into the Labyrinth crumbled from lack of maintenance, like Greek society since austerity began. Moisture seeped through cement and trickled down cracks, little rivulets that nibbled at the foundations. Dim light with no visible source reduced everything to a uniform grey. He could detect no sign of the concealed cameras.

An image of Phaedra's golden curls flashed into his mind. He tripped on a broken cobblestone and fell to one knee.

He swore, inspecting the skin beneath the torn denim. A dirty shallow graze, no blood. Lucky. *Keep your mind on the prize, Theseus. She's not the prize.* He stood and his knee twinged.

Where were the other contestants? Contestants entered two by two, and then the Minotaur was released. It was unlikely they had deviated from that format.

"If it's rigged, who are they most likely to save?" he asked himself. Not me. He pushed the thought of lovely eyes and golden curls out of his mind.

There would be caches of food scattered around the Labyrinth, and maybe some small weapons. Nothing big enough to seriously wound the Minotaur. He stopped in the corridor, closed his eyes and listened. *Drip drip* ahead of him, nothing else. Instinct told him to wait.

Rapid breathing, shallow and high. Rocks skittered over the stony floor. *Not the Minotaur.*

The person rounded a corner and saw Theseus. It was a boy his own age, of average height and slender build, skin pale in the grey light. His black hair was short and styled into spikes.

"Who are you?" the boy called.

Theseus waved. "Theseus. Come, hurry."

The boy hurried to his side. *Naïve.* Theseus felt a prickle of guilt. *I don't know him. A necessary sacrifice.*

You keep telling yourself that, a nastier voice inside his head said.

'My name's Dion. Man, I almost hurled when that scream . . . Hey, you gotta smoke?' The boy stank of vomit.

Theseus clenched his teeth together. "No."

"Yeah, figures. They took mine, too. You'd think they'd let us smoke if we're gonna die, anyway." Dion shrugged and spread his hands out.

"You think you're going to die?"

"I didn't last night, above ground, with those people cheering me and the bright lights and cameras. Oh, yeah, mate, I'm big, is what I thought. Now though . . . I'm just gonna run if I see the damn thing. Someone has to win, right?" He shivered.

They walked in silence. Far off, a choked cry. It ended sooner than the last.

"That's two," said Dion. "Sounds like it's a long way from us, too. Thank God."

Golden curls. *I hope it wasn't her.*

Phaedra's legs were heavy. Walking tired her quicker than she expected. *It's just the fear,* she told herself. If she held her hands up with fingers spread they shook, so she kept them clenched in fists.

They liked me. They promised.

Her Mama's voice berated her in her mind. "Phaedra, what is this nonsense? You crazy? I forbid it."

"I'm eighteen, Mama. You can't stop me." Her lip had trembled; she had wanted to run from Mama's anger. "I signed already. I'll be famous." *And we'll have money for your medicine.*

"You'll be *dead,* my darling. My baby girl. How could you do this to me?" Mama had sunk into a chair, covered her eyes with her hands and wailed like she was already dead. Phaedra had crept out of the room; she hadn't spoken to her Mama since.

Last season the winner got a modelling contract. Guaranteed work. Good pay. Mama needed her medicine.

The producers liked her. It was settled.

Dark eyes peered into her soul. *It's not rigged, you know.*

Maybe Theseus was right, and those producers were sitting in their chairs laughing at her right now.

A sudden chill brought goose bumps to speckle her skin. She approached a corner, slowed and stopped.

"What's that?" A voice echoed in the underground maze, but she was sure it came from around the corner. There was nothing behind her but fetid air. She held her breath.

"'Shh, I heard something," it said again. A female voice. Phaedra stayed frozen. To reveal herself or not? She edged forward, but halted at a different sound.

A snort beyond the corner. Phaedra turned and ran.

Screams followed her, incoherent words.

Something pursued her, either the beast or one of the contestants. *Don't look,* she chanted in her head. *Just keep running.* She willed her aching legs faster.

"Stop," a different voice called, a human voice. She slowed to a jog and looked back over her shoulder. A boy covered in blood limped down the gloomy corridor. "Help me," he said.

From the gloom behind him a monstrous shadow rose up.

Adrenaline flooded her muscles as her nostrils filled with an earthy, musty bull smell. As she turned to run, a wall to her right shifted, sliding across to reveal a pitch-black recess. Without hesitation Phaedra lunged and the panel slid across, sealing her in.

The wall muffled the boy's cries. In the silence that followed she heard snuffling and scratching on the other side of her hiding place. Huddled on the ground Phaedra prayed, completely blind. The noises ceased, and after a while the wall shifted again to let her out.

It's not rigged, you know.

After the absolute blackness of the secret room the dimly lit corridor was bright, and she squinted up and down. The room sealed back up; in moments the hidden door was invisible.

It's totally rigged.

It was hard to judge the passage of time underground, but Theseus's best guess was that half a day had passed since the door had opened to let them into the Labyrinth. He and Dion stumbled upon a cache of snacks: chocolate bars, packets of chips, a few cans of warm soda. They devoured the junk in a few minutes, leaving plastic and cans where they fell.

"We should move," Theseus said but Dion wanted to rest. He leaned back against the wall and rubbed his belly.

"Just a few more minutes," he said, groaning.

Theseus bit back a nasty reply and waited, tapping his foot and rubbing the silky hairs at the end of his braid between his fingertips. Finally Dion staggered to his feet.

"Man, we gotta sleep at some point."

"Yes. But not here. We'll find a better place and one can keep watch while the other sleeps." Theseus gazed along the passage. "Let's keep going this way."

The maze twisted and turned like a frenzied snake, doubling back and ending suddenly with increasing frequency. Dead-ends forced them to retreat four times. At the next long stretch of corridor, Theseus announced a rest stop.

"We're totally exposed here."

Theseus nodded. "But we can see anyone—or anything—coming at us. We aren't boxed in and we can run the other way. This is as good as it gets in here." He sat with his legs crossed. "I'll take first watch."

Dion curled up with his back to the wall and fell asleep. In repose the boy looked younger than eighteen.

Why did you audition? Phaedra had asked.

In Theseus's memory it was his eighth winter: snow covered the house his family lived in. He saw his brother, Nicos, come walking along the path, head down, framed by skeletal trees that stood black against the blank sky. In his little-boy excitement he ran and jumped on his big brother's back, but Nicos had brushed him off with barely a word. Much later, he learned that Nicos' wife had died in childbirth. Because of the austerity measures the hospital wouldn't let Nicos see the baby, a son, until he paid for the care she received. Laid off two months before, Nicos had no money. So he walked from the hospital, all the way from the city, and came home. He left the baby behind. By the time Mama and Papa got to the hospital the baby had been made a ward of the state and "adopted" out—sold, rather—to cover the hospital's costs. But eight-year old Theseus wasn't told this at the time; all he knew was that something had happened to his brother, who he adored, and it had something to do with the government.

He stared at Dion's smooth face. *I'm doing it for my nephew. For my brother. For all the Greek people.*

That didn't make it any easier.

He woke Dion when his eyelids threatened to glue themselves shut. Sleep claimed him quickly.

A kick in the ribs woke him; he grunted and rolled away.

"Sorry, you were talking," Dion said. He looked up and down the corridor,up and down, down and up. "You hear that last scream? How many's that make?"

"No, I must have slept through it." He rubbed gritty eyes and yawned. The soda had left a bitter aftertaste and his teeth were furry. "I don't feel like I slept at all."

Dion nodded and ran a hand through his hair. The spikes were worse for wear after his sleep—no gel to style them in the Labyrinth.

"Let's keep moving, then."

They found two skinny teenage girls cowering in a dead end that reeked of urine. Theseus begged them to stand up and move, but they shook their heads. "We'll be safer here," the shorter one said with staring eyes, though couldn't answer when he asked why. He flung his hands up and they left them to their fate.

"Stupid," Dion said. "I wonder why they bothered to audition."

"Same reason as you, maybe. The girl I was in the cell with—" *her name is Phaedra* "—she said fame. Fame, stardom, the chance at a better life—those are the usual reasons, right?"

"Yeah." Dion scratched the stubble on his chin. "But those girls, they were broken. Like, you know what you're signing up for. Why face it like that?"

"It's one thing to see it on TV, it's another to live it. It's all about the winners, on TV. The meal ticket out of austerity."

Dion watched his feet as they walked. "I guess."

Movement at the next corner alerted them. The figure was too small to be the Minotaur, so they relaxed their guard. Only a bit. Contestants had been known to tip the odds in their favour by injuring weaker contestants, making them easier targets for the Minotaur. One winner had been dubbed the Hamstringer, for his crippling attacks on other contestants.

Golden curls.

"Theseus?" she called before he could speak.

"Phaedra."

"You know her?" Dion asked, eyebrows high.

"The girl from the cell," Theseus replied, taking her appearance in as they got close. Her hair was tangled and dirty, her face and clothes smeared with filth. The subtle eye makeup had run, staining the skin around her eyes with darkness. She was unhurt, he noted with a sense of lightness. She met his gaze briefly then looked away.

"Are you okay?" she said, nodding at his knee.

"Yeah, just a scratch. Haven't seen the Minotaur. Have you?"

She paused, glancing up at the ceiling. "In the distance. He killed two people while I ran away."

"Oh." Theseus looked at Dion, saw him staring at Phaedra. What was that in his expression? Mistrust? Hostility? He stepped forward and put his body between them. "You're welcome to walk with us."

"Walk where? Where are you going, Theseus? All roads lead to the Minotaur," she said and laughed without humour.

"We're safer in a group. Please." He stretched out a hand. Dion coughed behind him. She glanced over his shoulder at Dion, then back the way she had come.

"Okay."

Phaedra fell behind as they walked, watching the sway of Theseus's dark braid. His jeans were snug and showed off his taut rear. *Nice,* she thought, then blushed.

She wondered how far away the girl with the knife was. A small, lithe girl, with olive skin and black hair in a braid similar to the one Theseus wore, clutching a shiny dagger.

The dagger lay on a concrete plinth in a dead end. Phaedra approached cautiously, unsure if it was a trap. She would have preferred to find a food cache, her belly so empty it gnawed at itself. As she edged forward something shoved her from behind and she sprawled across the floor, catching her shoulder painfully on the plinth.

A flash of dark eyes, a black braid, the dagger poised above her; the girl stared down at her, then with a sharp exhalation whirled and ran.

Her stomach growled at her, loud enough that Theseus glanced back to see what the noise was. She gave him a half-smile. "Hungry." The rotten smell of the enclosed corridor mingled with a musky scent that tugged her memory.

Scrabbling sounds, snorts.

From a hidden corner the Minotaur charged.

Phaedra caught a glimpse of red eyes and two sharply curved horns before Theseus pushed her back and she fell to the ground, twisting her wrist. She rolled over and scrambled to her feet, swearing, and saw Theseus trip Dion as he tried to bolt. The Minotaur grabbed Dion's neck and lifted him high. Phaedra's mouth hung open, transfixed by the beast, but movement caught her eye. She saw Theseus fiddle with the end of his braid, and while the Minotaur was occupied he ducked in under a spray of blood and hit the Minotaur with his bare hand.

What is he doing?

The Minotaur stumbled; Theseus backed away, dripping with gore. A panel shifted to Phaedra's left. She hurled herself forward, grabbed Theseus and hauled him into the secret room. The door slammed shut as the Minotaur charged—it hit with brute force. The wall shook and grit fell on them.

"What the hell?" she snapped. "What did . . . why did . . . ? You tripped him!"

"Shh," he said.

She struggled to slow her breathing; the Minotaur made no sound. Theseus tried to wipe the congealing blood away, but only succeeded in smearing it. The metallic smell invaded Phaedra's nostrils. After a long pause Theseus said, "I had a poisoned toothpick in my braid."

Theseus fiddling with his hair, slamming the Minotaur with his hand.

"A poisoned toothpick?"

"I soaked it in a synthetic nerve agent. I wasn't sure how long it would take to work on the Minotaur—it works on humans in a few seconds."

Her head throbbed. "You killed it? The boy was . . . "

She imagined she could hear his smile. "A delaying tactic. I killed it, yes."

A delaying tactic. Was that what he had planned for me? He'd beckoned, at the door leading to the Labyrinth. *"Are you coming?"* he'd said. She slumped back against the wall and sighed.

His hand found hers and gripped it tight.

Minos shook his head at the infra-red vision on the screen. "Dumb fools," he muttered as he pressed a button in the control panel in front of him. "You think you're the first ones to kill the Minotaur?"

He switched his gaze to a different screen. The black-and-white monitor showed a steel drawer opening, the hydraulics jerky but functional. The Meat Lockers, as they were affectionately known, housed the replacements.

"Vitals look good," Minos said into his headpiece, and a white-coated woman walked into view on the screen. She checked the eight-foot long body that lay supine in the cold chamber drawer. The body of a naked man surmounted by the massive head of a bull.

"Ready when you are," Minos said. The woman found a vein in the creature's arm and slid the needle under the skin. She pushed the contents of the syringe into the body and stepped back. Minos kept an eye on his computer monitor.

"Time to go," he said after thirty seconds and the woman exited the screen. Minos watched as the body on the screen stirred, lifted its ungainly head. Frankenstein's monster lived. The eyes opened wide and nostrils flared. It tried to sit up, but was unbalanced and fell to the ground. The creature shook its head and rose slowly to its feet, chest heaving, glaring around the cold room as it gained control over its top-heavy body. Muscles flexed.

Minos looked back to the monitor where two young people full of hope and life crouched together. "Showtime," he said with a smile as the woman from the cold room sat down beside him. She leaned over and pulled a lever. They watched Theseus and Phaedra scramble away from the door that opened, but after poking his head out Theseus gestured for Phaedra to follow him.

Minos switched camera views. "I think that's long enough."

"I feel a bit bad for them," the woman said as she pressed a green button.

"You do?" Minos screwed his face up. On the black-and-white screen the new Minotaur sniffed at the open space where moments before there had been a wall. "Go on, out you go." The beast lunged forward, out of view. Minos stared at the empty room then swapped to the hall cameras.

"They made their choice."

Theseus stopped in the corridor, so abrupt that Phaedra bumped into his back. "Did you hear that?" he asked.

Phaedra frowned and tilted her head. She shrugged.

A snort.

Theseus turned and looked down into her face. It mirrored his shock.

"Theseus—" she said but he shoved her away from him.

"Run. Live."

She hesitated, her face contorting. Then she thrust out her jaw and shook her head. "Don't tell me what to do, Theseus."

Side by side they clasped sweaty hands and braced themselves for the onslaught.

"The winner of the sixteenth Labyrinth Hope is . . . Ariadne!"

A roar from the crowd swelled as the small girl with the dark braid trudged across the sand, blinded by the floodlights. The host, a glamorous woman with long honey-coloured hair, took her by the hand and led her to an ornate throne. The girl blinked and stumbled as she sat.

"So, Ariadne, tell me—how do you feel?"

The girl squinted around the restored Theatre of Dionysus, packed with cheering people, then at the host. A montage of the show's "highlights" were replayed on huge screens. She recognized the girl with the golden curls. *Not so pretty now.*

Her lips twitched in a satisfied grin as she leaned back against the throne.

"Great. I won."

The screen cut to commercials.

Roxanne

Amanda Lara

When I spin for the last time, I'm thinking about The White Stripes, and how Eric would have loved it if I had used one of their songs for the competition routine. As the edges of the rink blur, and I try desperately to maintain my focal point—the crimson *U* of Underwood Skating Centre, spray-painted on one of the concrete walls in boxy letters—the bass of "Seven Nation Army" continues to reverberate within the hollows of my skull. Taken out of context, it's a haunting noise, especially since I'm alone until five-thirty. The new girl in the club, Kimberly Jones, has her session right after mine; so far, she's been terrifyingly punctual.

The faint strains of the strumming bass grow louder, and I skid the blade of my skate against the ice. The sharp buzz of the ice being shaven clears the eerie beat away instantly, and I'm left at a standstill, breathing hard. Through the smudged Plexiglas, the fluorescent EXIT sign burns vigilantly, and I note for the thousandth time that the light is green rather than red.

I can't do this right now. Even the voice in my head sounds miserable.

But Eric's been dead for a month, and the competition was two weeks ago. My excuses are becoming invalid, especially to Coach. Fragments of our last conversation wafts into my train of thought, and I wince recalling the disappointment in her tone.

"The Olympics are over, Maddy . . . I'm proud that you made it as far

as you did, but it's in the past now. You're eighteen . . . you're still young. Time to move on."

I'd never told her about Eric's dying wish, the one about me carrying the gold medal to his grave and showing it to the tombstone. It was morbid, but he had been thirteen, and all thirteen-year-old boys liked that kind of thing. Never mind the tumor in his brain, never mind the months of chemotherapy that did nothing to save his life, never mind that I hadn't even won a medal of any kind to bring to him in death.

Damn it.

I dig my palms into my forehead, struggling not to let the shame overwhelm me. At this point, I no longer care how much time I have left—I can no longer breathe in this wintery, cool air, because it stings the interior of my sick stomach.

Turning heel, I pivot in the direction of the opposite side of the rink, where the exit is and—

There's someone on the ice.

Startled, I nearly slip as I'm trying to halt, and stumble into the barrier and Plexiglas.

Jesus, what is this guy doing here? Instantly, annoyance bubbles underneath my nerves. This time is private—no unauthorized person is supposed to be here. If it were any other day, I would be all right with someone making a mistake, but it's today, and suddenly I'm irritated with the stranger that is cutting into the session I had been so desperate to leave only a few seconds ago.

"Excuse me!" I wave and push myself off the barrier, speeding toward the figure. "I'm sorry, but you're not supposed to be here! I'm training right now!"

For a split second, I wonder if the figure is Kimberly, but the theory evaporates when I get closer. The figure is clearly a man—he's far too tall to be Kim—and he's not wearing any skates, not even the kind a hockey player would use, and yet he's standing in the middle of the rink. His dark trench coat seems hardly appropriate for a hockey practice, anyway, and there's a thick yellow scarf wrapped around his neck, making it hard to see his face.

Unease pierces a hole in my chest, so I skid to a stop when I'm a few feet away.

"Sir, I'm sorry, but this is a private practice. I don't know why the guys at the front let you in, but the rest of the night is for the club skaters. I'm sure they could get you a refund or something."

"Hey there, Roxanne," the man says calmly, but he's not looking at me. Judging from the angle of his neck, I think he's staring at the blue lines beneath the ice, used for the hockey games.

Either way, the name sparks my irritation, even if he didn't mean it. Roxanne was the name of the girl who'd won the gold medal in Women's Individual Figure Skating, for a routine to Beethoven's Fifth Symphony.

"My name's not Roxanne," I correct him, attempting to withhold the bite in my tone, "And there's no girl on the club named Roxanne. Are you sure she's here?"

"Didn't you win the gold for figure skating?"

Now I *am* flabbergasted, not to mention offended, and make no effort to conceal my contempt. "No, sir, Roxanne Swanson is from Canada. Don't you watch TV? Or read the newspapers? Or go on the Internet? I don't look anything like her."

The skin of his cheek pulls, and I imagine him smirking under the yellow fabric.

"Shame."

Shame that I wasn't the girl he was asking for, or shame on me for not being her? God, he was creeping me out.

"Sir, I'm going to have to get someone if you don't leave immediately." My voice is snappish, and I fold my arms across my chest. The muscles in my thighs are growing sore from keeping still, so I drift toward the exit, and turn expectantly toward him as I do so.

But he's already moved across the ice, despite not wearing skates, and I'm quick to leap off the rink and onto the rubbery, dry ground. A vending machine hums behind me, and I'm reminded of The White Stripes' bass; once again, the memory of the rhythm bothers me, and I suppress a shudder.

The man glides off the ice with such an impressive grace, I'm stunned. People tend to stumble off the slick surface *with* skates, much less in boots. Shrinking into the Plexiglas wall, I manage to splutter,

"Thank you for your understanding."

The man tugs down the yellow scarf, leaving his face unobstructed. Blood roars in my ears, because he looks *just like* Eric, if Eric had lived to see twenty-something, but *oh, my* God he has his eyebrows and his nose and his chin and his deep green eyes—

"See you later, Roxanne."

Up until he'd spoken, I am positive I'd been making some strange, dumbstruck expression from the eeriness of it all. But the name *Roxanne* jars me out of it, and I blurt out, "Jesus Christ, I'm *not* Roxanne!"

Immediately, I cover my mouth, horrified. But Eric's lookalike has already turned and floated away. The impulse to ask the man what his name is lingers longingly on my lips, and once again, I'm left at a standstill.

"Hey, babe, what's a-shaking?"

Kimberly Jones is shoving her gym bag into the locker across from mine. Tugging out her earbuds and wrapping them around her pink MP3 player, she glances back at me when I don't respond.

"Babe, you look kind of sick. Is everything okay?"

No.

"Yeah, um," I clear my throat. "I think I ate something bad. I'm trying to figure out what it was."

"Oh, Maddy."

I hoist my foot up on a bench, knowing it might damage the blade of the skate, and not caring a single bit.

"Some guy walked in during my session," I say, trying to keep my tone conversational. "I can't believe the guys at the front let him through." My fingers are shaking, barely able to pull the weathered laces out of their knots.

Kimberly is winding her thin, golden hair into a top-bun, a couple of bobby pins hanging off the corner of her lips like tiny black cigarettes. Her doughy eyes enlarge, taking up nearly half her face.

"Whaa?" She splutters through the bobby pins. One falls to the floor with a pleasant *clink*, and she hastily bends down to pick it up.

The skate is having a hard time getting off my foot. Sweat from my workout has starting to run down into my eyelids, probably ruining my makeup; I wipe the underside of each eye and sniffle a little bit.

"Yeah. He went onto the rink without skates and everything."

The temptation to blurt out the truth—*he looked just like Eric*—flounders in my throat. What would she say if I told her? Would she believe me?

"What the hell?" Kim agrees, eyeing her phone one more time before slamming the locker door shut. I tug off my other skate, listening to the lull of the air conditioner, unable to form a coherent sentence.

I do not tell her the truth. Instead, I carefully place my skates into my gym bag, mutter a quick goodbye and leave the locker room.

However, I make sure to go through the front entrance. An overweight man with a graying mustache is eagerly tapping the screen of his phone. The perky soundtrack of whatever game he is playing echoes against the concrete walls, grating at my nerves.

"Excuse me, sir," I say. The words are polite in themselves, but they drip with an irritation I cannot taper. The man glances up from his phone and gives me a long, lazy look, which provokes me further.

"Look, I'm a club skater for this rink, and I have a private session from four-thirty to five-thirty. No one else is allowed in the rink. Isn't that why you're here? To keep out people?"

The man frowns. "Miss, no one came in. I would've seen 'em."

"Were you playing your game?" My voice is testy. Today is not the day for this.

Now the offense is blatant on the man's face. "Miss, I can assure you, *no one came in.*"

A chill traces my spine. Why is he lying?

"I'm going to speak with your boss." I retort, but the last syllable shakes. Kimberly was right—*what the hell?* Before the man can answer, I swing around and head into the parking lot. It's empty, save for Kim's car, the man at the office's and mine. In the darkness, the space seems to swallow me. For a minute I simply stand there, queasy, staring into the night.

In the back of my mind, the beat of that damn song begins to tick again.

Roxanne Swanson has red hair; that much I remember about her the entire drive home, and I even think about it when my mother kisses me at the door.

She asks me how my day was, and I dare not tell her about Eric's doppelgänger. She lost my father to a drunk driver during my infancy, and the death of her preteen son had barely left her alive. Such news would destroy her—she would think her daughter had been driven to madness.

Dinner is a quiet event. She asks me how practice went, and I tell her it went fine, as always. I wonder if she believes me now, since I didn't win any medals. I'm glad she doesn't bring up college registration tonight. How many times could I say it—*I don't want to go to college, I want to focus on skating*—before she took me seriously? Eric had been the one for college, all into science and cutting up frogs, dreaming about things that I'd never wanted.

I go upstairs, shower and, once I'm settled, I grab my laptop. Before I can stop myself, my fingers are typing *Roxanne Swanson* into the search engine and clicking on the *Images* option. The first picture that appears is of her winning the gold medal; the mere memory of the unhappiness I'd felt causes nausea. Swallowing, I push the sensation away and scrutinize the photograph, searching for similarities between us. We're both fair-skinned, perhaps around the same height, but that is where any form of resemblance ends. As I'd remembered, Roxanne's hair is a deep, rich red that falls a little past her shoulders. My own locks are wavy and dark, stretching to elbow length. Roxanne has green eyes; I have brown. Roxanne has a gold medal; I have nothing.

Zooming in on the photograph, I also notice that one of her teeth—a canine—is broken in half, leaving a little dark hole at the side of her smile.

At this point I'm reaffirming my discredit toward the mysterious man from the rink, because I really *do* look nothing like Roxanne Swanson, and there is no way he could have mistaken me for her. He really *was* simply a malicious bastard, and I resolve to call for help if he ever intrudes on my session again.

Unwillingly, I glance at a framed photograph on my nightstand, one that contains a faded picture of Eric and I only a few years back. It was taken at one of my competitions, one where I *had* won first place. I was twelve, maybe thirteen, wearing a sparkling pink costume that is still lost somewhere in the back of my closet. Eric was around seven or eight, his hair still a strange hazel color as the traces of childhood towhead began to grow out. The only real memory I've retained from that particular event is that Eric had told me he was afraid that I would fall and my tongue would stick on the ice, and that another skater would run over it by accident and cut my tongue off. My father had taken away Eric's video games for a week, but I haven't really thought about the incident too much since.

The photograph had really captured the vibrant green of Eric's eyes, and they seem to hold me until I turn out the lights.

I'm working on my new routine. Coach has just left, and she'd worked me hard today. I'm doing the choreography to a tango number—nothing by The White Stripes, which is a bit of a relief. It's my alone time, the private session, and I skate the length of the rink furiously before trying one of the leaps.

Just as I'm about to leave the ground, something dark catches the corner of my eye. Frightened, I slip and slam into the ice. Pain ricochets under my thighs, and I'm spitting curses into the ground.

"You okay, Roxanne?"

I see the fabric of his pants before I even look up—how does he move so fast? I scuttle backward, hissing through the agony.

"You're not supposed to be here! I told you that yesterday!"

Eric's eyes illuminate, and the man raises his gloved hands in defense.

"Sorry, Roxanne. I didn't mean to scare you."

"Stop calling me that!"

I wince; the effort it has taken to shout filters all the way into my injured thighs.

"Calling you what?" The man frowns. "'Roxanne'? Isn't that your name?"

"No." I pant, struggling to rise.

"I thought you had won the gold for me."

Those words induce a horrible, terrible chill in my heart.

Damn it all. I'll crawl away if I have to.

"Get away from me, you creep," I say through my teeth, propping myself onto my elbows and beginning to drag myself across the rink.

The world suddenly shrinks beneath me; Eric's doppelgänger has lifted me up, toting me to the exit. Fear clenches my stomach, and I begin to scratch at his trench coat.

"Let me go! Let me go! *Help me! Someone help me!*"

The man only laughs.

He settles on a bench once we are off the rink and sits me down on his lap, ignoring my cries. Without warning, he removes a glove and jams his hand under my thigh, massaging the bruised area. I'm so shocked, my voice simply gives out, and I only stare dumbly at the twenty-something duplicate of my brother as he feels my leg.

"I don't think it's anything serious," he concludes after a few moments, giving me a sideways grin. "But you might have to stay off the rink for a day or two."

I don't reply. It's like there's a ghostly finger painting a line down my spine—up and down, up and down, up and down.

Eric's eyebrows tip, and it's strange to see how grown-up the familiar gesture seems on a man's face.

"C'mon, Roxanne. I told you I was sorry. I really didn't mean to scare you."

His hand is still under my thigh, warm and close.

"Who are you?" My voice is hardly above a whisper.

The worry vanishes from his expression, immediately replaced with an eerie seriousness.

"You already know that."

I shake my head, rapidly. "No, I don't."

A smile stretches across his face, and the doppelgänger kisses me on the mouth. I exhale sharply when he pulls at my bottom lip, pulling me in closer, pulling me under—

I yank my mouth away, gasping. "You can't be him! You're not Eric! Eric died when he was *thirteen!* Eric is *dead!* Who the hell *are you?*"

Eric's lookalike is unfazed. "Oh, come *on*, Roxanne—"

"I'm not Roxanne Swanson! My name is *Mad—*"

Eric cuts me off with another kiss, but this time I jerk away instantly and strike him across the cheek.

"Put me down! Get away from me! Go away! Go away!"

I hear a sigh, feel my bottom being dropped onto the rubber-wire bench, and watch his feet glide away from me, out the front exit.

My mother said it was only bruising, and Coach said she'd seen worse, but both agreed that I take the next week off. Privately, I agreed with both of them, and couldn't have been more grateful for the distance between myself and the skating centre that I am now sorely convinced is haunted. By what sort of entity haunts it is still up in the air—is it a shape-shifting ghoul? A deity? I've even considered the possibility of a drug-induced hallucination, even if the most I take daily is aspirin.

Kimberly asks me to go out for coffee after her practice a few days into my break. I sit on the sidelines and watched her routine, then drive us to the nearest café.

"Babe, you're limping. Are you sure you're okay?"

"Yeah," I grimace as I stare at the daily specials. No matter what I do, the memory of the man's lips on mine refuses to fade. "You can go first."

Kim shrugs and steps forward, ordering a cappuccino. Absent-mindedly, I realize that the beat of "Seven Nation Army" has begun to filter back into my train of thought. Or is that my heartbeat? The white chalk letters on the menu are starting to blur together—I shake my head and quickly replace Kim when she moves out of the way.

"G-green tea latte, please," I stammer, doing my best to blink away the haze.

"Name?" The barista asks politely, poising a Sharpie over the paper cup.

A beat passes, and I blurt out, "Roxanne."

It's too late to correct myself—the girl is already inscribing *Roxanne* in bold, large font at the side of the cup, and smoothly hands it off to another worker. I can feel Kimberly's stare bore into the back of my head, and I don't move until someone requests me to.

It's only a few more days before I can go back on the rink, and all I can feel is a strange, buoyant anticipation froth within the bottom of my stomach.

"Mom?" I'm staring at my reflection and tugging at the splintered, dry ends of my hair.

"Hmm?" She replies from the laundry room, only a few paces away.

"I think I need a haircut."

"Okay. Call and see if Gina's in today."

"Can I . . . Can I dye my hair red?"

This catches her attention, and she appears in the bathroom doorway with a full bin of laundry and a flabbergasted expression scrawled across her features.

"Why on *Earth* would you want to do that? Your hair is beautiful just the way it is!"

"I-I just want to try out a different look, that's all."

She huffs, rolling her dark eyes as she readjusts the laundry basket. "Honestly? I think you need to be worrying more about college and less on your hair."

Anger sparks within me faster than a bullet train. "Mom, we've already talked about this! I'm not going to college, I'm going to focus on my skating, and I'm going to go to the next Olympics—"

"And do *what* after?" My mother yells, hair frizzing out of her bun. "You can only skate for so long, Maddy. You need a degree!"

"Oh, my God!" I shriek, itching to rip her throat open. "You're just disappointed that *I'm not* Eric! You always wanted me to get some—some freaking PhD like Eric dreamed of! Just admit it!"

She goes still.

"Don't you make this about Eric," she whispers dangerously, pointing a quivering finger in my direction, "or I'm going to come over there and smack you."

But I'm already crying, shutting the bathroom door and sinking to the floor, dimly wondering how much store-bought hair dye costs.

It's four in the morning, and I'm supposed to meet Coach at the rink by 6:00 o'clock. She's spending the whole day with me to make up for the lost time, which I'm okay with, because my mother and I haven't spoken since our argument.

Darkness shrouds my bathroom, yet somehow, it is comforting. I'm reluctant to turn on the light, and wince when the yellow bulb flickers and coats the room in its garish glow.

As I'm tying my hair into a bun, I smile experimentally to check for stray particles of food. Finishing the bun, I scoot closer to the bathroom mirror to make sure everything is clear, rotating my head back and forth and inspecting all angles.

Abruptly, I stop. The canine on the left side of my mouth shines innocently under the bathroom light, taunting me.

My body is moving out of the bathroom, toward the front door, into the garage—there, in a dusty corner, is a box filled with my father's old tools, sitting untouched after many years.

Robotically, I open it, rummaging through screwdrivers and nails until I find one: a tiny hammer, worn and dirty from its glory days. I'm carrying the tool back into the house, not making a sound, right back into the bathroom, where I close and lock the door.

There, I pull back the upper part of my lip with one hand, poising the hammer in the other, and focusing on the glimmering, whole tooth reflected in the mirror.

Coach is squinting at me when I glide onto the rink. Her gaze is wary.

"Good morning. You feeling okay?"

I smile brightly back, circling around her.

"Good morning. And thanks, I feel great."

She purses her lips.

"What did you do to your hair?"

"This?" I point to the bun. "I did it last night. I wanted to try something . . . better, you know?"

Coach is biting her lip, something bizarre pinching at her face.

"Hon, Kimberly told me what happened the other day, when you two went out for coffee."

I hoist my leg into the air, sparing only a swift glance back at Coach, who's trailing behind me.

"What happened?"

"She said that you told the barista your name was Roxanne."

"So?"

"Stop, Maddy." Irritation is scraping Coach's tone, and I comply, twisting back around to face her. The woman's aged, worn-out face is painted with concern.

"Maybe you need to take a break for a little bit longer. I'm going to call your mother right now."

Right away, I'm furious—I can't go back home, and I can't stand a moment more with my mother. The rink is my true home.

"I don't understand, Coach!" My voice cracks. "Why can't I stay and practice?"

"Because!" She bursts out, gesturing desperately to my figure. "Look at you! You—you colored your hair red! Kim said you called yourself Roxanne! I don't know what the *hell* is going on, but it's not okay! Is this *guilt* for not winning the gold? Okay, Maddy, I understand you were upset—"

"Don't call me Maddy," I interject, annoyed.

She sucks in a sharp, surprised breath. "Is that a *space* in your mouth?"

Silence reverberates in between us. Eventually, I smile.

"I'm calling your mother." Coach is turning heel and speeding off the rink. My irritation subsides with the buzz of her skates on the ice, echoing against the Plexiglas.

Swallowing, I put my hands in a loop before my body, move a bit for momentum, and begin to spin. The *U* winks through the blur every few seconds, and I'm not surprised to hear the bass of The White Stripes' song return when he does.

"You look beautiful, Roxanne." Eric says in the whirlwind, the white of his smile twisting as the world moves around me.

"I have your medal for you," I remark, not stopping. Dizziness is beginning to take my brain, but I continue without hesitation.

"Good. We can take it to my grave."

My arms and thighs are burning, but I am above the stars right now, because Eric is with me. Eric is *here*—

"Roxanne."

"Yes?" I pant.

"You know what to do."

I stumble, fall on my chest, feel pain riot up my figure, watch a pair of feet, wearing neon-green skates, rush toward me, open my mouth willingly, and see red, red everywhere. Someone is screaming, I feel nothing, and the strumming bass has grown deep and warped, playing on repeat in my brain.

The Goblin

Llanwyre Laish

Summer

In the summer, when Johanna was like everyone else with a life planned out from cradle to grave, she laughed at the goblin.

Each day he perched alongside the road between the village and the market fair. An absurd, twisted, green creature with a sparse tuft of black hair on his head, the goblin sat in the moist grass and lectured endlessly to a rock he clutched in his hand. Even his rock was unattractive: it was craggy and remained covered with dirt no matter how hard it rained. He called it his "lovely friend," and sometimes he would yell at it, but most days, he simply lectured.

His lectures ran the gamut from how the rock should comport itself to how one might care for a horse that took sick in the rain. The clever goblin knew many useful things from sitting alongside the road, for carts often backed up along the narrow path and merchants would stand for hours discussing their wares and trades next to the listening creature. He internalized what he heard and then digested it for the rock's benefit, delivering his knowledge in a high, harsh voice. He punctuated particularly important points by banging his fist on the ground.

Most people from the village ignored the goblin, although those who drank late into the night at the tavern often made him the butt of jokes when they wearied of gossiping about their neighbours. Poking fun at the goblin always seemed too easy, though; when they were children and Johanna and her brother would laugh at him, their mother would shake her head and simply say, "Low-hanging fruit."

By that summer, though, Johanna was no longer a child. Her father had died the previous spring, and as the only apprentice he'd ever had, she'd had to step into her father's place as head of the Wheat Grower's Guild. She taught people in all five of the local villages how best to tend their crops and store grain in the winter, helped them manage trading at the fair, and brought them all together at high festivals to compete in games against the other guilds, which they invariably lost but always enjoyed. In her father's guild people laughed and they all took care of one another; she meant to keep it that way. It looked like a good harvest that year, so all five of the villages would have extra grain to put back in case of a hard winter. The taverns were filled with laughter and warmth, and everyone looked forward to a good season of rest.

Even the goblin picked up the theme and lectured the rock about the need for a good winter's rest. His thin patch of hair swayed gently in the breeze as he raised his fist in the air, furious about those with the audacity *not* to rest when they should. Johanna smiled to herself when she caught his lecture and carried on with her trip to the market, exhausted by the continual work but happy to serve.

Fall

In the fall, Johanna first listened to the goblin.

She and her assistant, whose name was Jack, carted a load full of the village's metal farming equipment to the fair for repair before the final harvest. The rain fell heavy and cold, making huge holes in the packed earth, and her cartwheel caught in a rut and broke right next to the road's sharp turn into the forest.

The goblin sat just near the tree line, chewing on a wad of grass. He watched Johanna and Jack curiously as they cursed and managed the horses. He sidled up like a child, not ever looking directly at them. He stared at the wheel, at the ground, at the horses, never quite approaching, but somehow getting closer nonetheless. In his knobby left hand he held his rock, which was covered in a thin layer of gooey mud. After a few minutes, he put it carefully down in the dying grass, patting it as though he worried that it would run away. He then came right up to the side of the road next to the cart and stood, silently looking at the ground, his hands clasped behind him.

They ignored him; the rain had already agitated the horses, and Johanna struggled to unhitch them in the downpour. Jack did his best to hold the broken wheel, which threatened to fall on him and make the heavy cart collapse. Despite her freezing fingers, Johanna finally got the horses loose and tied around a nearby tree and they began the process of taking one of the wooden crates from the back of the cart to prop up its bed so they could remove the wheel. It was arduous work; Johanna was small, and could barely get the huge crate out without crushing herself. Still, she was determined, and she managed to drag the crate down to the ground intact, and Jack had just put his shoulder under the edge of the cart so she could push the box under with her hip when she almost tripped over the goblin. He was barely as tall as the crate itself, but he'd braced himself and pushed with both his little hands to get the crate under the cart.

The crate barely moved.

Stifling laughter, Johanna put her hip to the crate and threw her body weight against it. It dug a long furrow in the dirt, but it went under. The goblin dusted his hands carefully, his wispy black hair slicked to his head by the rain. Without looking at either of them, he turned to leave the road again.

"Thank you!" she called after him. Jack gave Johanna a strange look.

The goblin stopped as though he'd been struck. He quivered there, still, his tattered little loincloth hanging sadly from his waist. He turned and looked at her directly for the first time. His eyes were wide and bright. "Nobody has ever *thanked* me before."

Somehow, his words moved Johanna. She'd heard odd little stories here and there in the village of the goblin's help; he was seldom effectual, but he always clearly meant well. As she'd joined the villagers in their cozy homes laughing about the silly little creature, it never occurred to her that these people offering up the stories had never thanked him for his sincere goodwill. She felt ashamed of herself, and embarrassed by the goblin's loneliness.

He continued to fix her with his strange little stare, patiently waiting for a response. She recognized her own loneliness in him, and her heart went out to him. "I'll bring you something from the market," she promised, "in return for the good deed you've done us." Jack rolled his eyes, but she ignored him.

The goblin's delight was palpable. He clapped his little hands, nodded and then turned to run crookedly to retrieve his rock. As he departed back into the forest, she could hear him recounting the story to it. "A gift! A real gift from the fair!"

The cart repair took a long time, and they reached the fair well after dark; they stayed that night in the temporary accommodations set up for just such emergencies, a gigantic tent littered with bedrolls. Jack quickly made himself popular by recounting their run-in with the goblin, and the drunken tradespeople who huddled in the tent laughed jovially at the goblin's expense. Their laughter annoyed Johanna; she went outside to sit by myself, and soon found their laughter encompassed her, too.

After she finished the trades and repairs the next day, Johanna carefully chose two gifts for the little goblin: a small loaf of sweet bread and a little string of blue glass beads, no more than a bracelet for a human, but enough to make a necklace for him. She wondered if she would find him on their return trip.

She needn't have worried; he stood at the turn where she'd found him the day before, his hands clasped patiently behind his back. For the first time, she saw him alert and scanning the roadway, and when he saw the cart, he raised his hand eagerly, then hesitantly pulled it back. She remembered the cruel laughter of the night before and wondered if he'd had people play tricks on him. Shooting a warning look at her assistant, Johanna raised her hand and gave the goblin an enthusiastic wave.

His little green face lit up and he gave an odd little jump. They pulled up to the side of the road, and she got down from the cart and then knelt down so she would be goblin height. Without speaking, she held out her two gifts, one in each palm. He snatched the bread eagerly and tucked it under one arm, grinning. Then he turned towards the little set of beads. His mouth hung open and he lifted them gingerly on one finger. He examined them, turning the bracelet around so he could touch each bead in turn, and then his eyes met hers. "Mine?" he asked.

She nodded. "For helping me."

He looked at Johanna solemnly. "Thank you." Still clutching the beads, he put his twisted little hand over his heart, and without another word, he turned and ran back into the woods, his loincloth drooping and bobbing as he ran.

"Gods," grumbled Jack as she got back into the cart. "Better check your pockets. Goblins are notorious thieves."

Winter

In the winter, Johanna and the goblin became friends.

The harvest went as well as promised, so the villages settled in for a winter of quiet celebration and rest. Now Johanna had time to herself, which she hadn't had since her father's death. It would do her good, everyone said. But it did the opposite. Johanna fretted and paced, unable to settle in one place for long. She arranged the canned fruits in the cellar by colour and then rearranged them alphabetically by contents. She swept and cleaned the floors until they shone, and repaired all the family's clothing and then all of the small spots of wear on the upholstery. She felt lonely, quiet, desolate; only movement kept her nervousness at bay, but eventually, she'd done everything she could but rest.

Her neighbours rested. The town rested. They held quiet dinners in celebration of a year's work well done. None of these relaxed gatherings pleased Johanna, who already yearned for another year of work. She could dimly remember when she hadn't been like this, but couldn't stop herself from pacing and wringing her hands.

She took to walking, putting on her heavy, hard boots, the ones her father had bought her for dealing with winter emergencies. She'd leave home for hours, roaming the roads around town, and when those stopped suiting her because of their familiarity, she wandered into the forest near the village, then to the outer forests. The villagers tutted, but blamed her restlessness on her grief.

Midway through winter, when snow had entirely covered the land, Johanna ran into the goblin on one of her walks. He had put the rock down in the snow, had run a few feet away and could no longer find it. When she came upon him, he was spinning in panicked circles, making anguished little cries. Johanna almost hid from him when she first saw him, thinking him a wounded animal, but then she saw the glint of green skin and recognized him. "Goodness," she said, stepping out from behind a tree and pulling her winter coat around her. "Whatever is wrong?"

The goblin looked up at her with earnest yellow eyes. "My rock," he said simply. His bottom lip quivered.

She nodded solemnly. She knew the pain of loss. "I'll help. Did you lose it nearby?"

Pained, the goblin could only nod.

They spent the better part of an hour searching the snow-covered forest floor. She wasn't sure she'd recognize the rock when she saw it, but she tried, anyway. The goblin stumbled along behind her, taking three steps for every one of hers. She felt calm, controlled and patient. She excelled at helping others.

It was finally the glint of blue that gave the rock away. She saw the unnatural colour near the root of a tree, unsure of what it was, and—not thinking that it had anything to do with the rock at all—approached to see who had lost what. Finding her beads beneath the tree startled her; had he lost them? Then she realized that they'd been perched on top of the rock, a strange tiara. Just as she'd understood, the goblin stumbled up to see what she'd seen and, with an overjoyed cry, leapt on the rock, hugging both rock and beads to his chest. He turned around with glee, shutting his eyes tight. When he opened them, they were filled with grateful tears.

She reached out and patted him gently on the shoulder. "There you go." She was happy to have helped someone today, even if it was only the strange little goblin. Perhaps she could rest tonight, she thought, and she did.

She met him again on her ramble the next day, although whether they met by chance or whether he waited for her, she could never tell. He fell into step beside her as best he could, and she slowed her pace. They walked in silence together for some time, and then they both erupted in a strange burst of speech that surprised both.

Johanna talked of life in the village and of the kinds of shining minutiae that stand out so clearly in the minds of those slowly pulled under by their sorrow: the light on the rows of canning jars in the early grey winter mornings, the way her younger brother's spoon clicked against the stone bowl he insisted on using, the endless preparations for winter festival which she stripped of all sense of community and boiled down to the endless cutting of paper for decorations. Instead of alarm or confusion, the goblin accepted her words with interest, his little yellow eyes growing wide as he heard about the festival customs or the fruits "trapped in glass."

In his turn, he told her disconnected little tales of his day, too: putting the rock in the water to clean it and seeing himself as though he had been under the water, waking to the rustle of migratory birds, angrily smashing with his bare hands a farmer's fence that should not have spoiled the view from his favourite hill. At times, he would punctuate his stories by waving the rock around, while at others, when he grew gentle, he would put his twisted little hand in Johanna's and they would walk along in silence for a few moments, their steps crunching in the snow. Often during the walk, the goblin would stop to polish the beads she'd given him, touching each one in turn between his forefinger and thumb, and it pleased her that he took such pleasure in them.

Johanna's walks turned longer and longer. Her family grew cross and the village started to whisper.

When she grew sick and could not go out for days, she fretted and cried, worrying that the goblin would miss her, or worse, that he would think that she had chosen not to join him. She was clever enough not to tell the others of this sorrow, though, and kept it inside. The doctor came and prescribed a month of rest in the house over winter festival. "Time with family will do her good," he assured her mother.

Time with family did exactly the opposite, however, and Johanna grew so angry and melancholy that her mother happily let her go back to her rambling as soon as she was able. The goblin waited patiently in a clearing near her house, and they took up again as though the lapse had never happened, falling into step and continuing their conversation of the week before as though it had never left off. Johanna felt relieved—nothing now seemed amiss. She felt safe and normal as the goblin told her a story of a blackbird caught in a tree, strangling to death with a dead vine caught around its neck.

The goblin admitted his obsession with the dead animals of the forest. He would often go to their corpses and poke them with a stick, removing the eyes from a rabbit or pulling a beak off a bird. He described these things in beautiful, loving language. Although those tales horrified Johanna, she took comfort in the fact that he always buried the animals afterwards. The goblin himself seemed pleased by the strangeness of his obsession, often marking it as making him different from "her people, who avoided death."

Yet she couldn't help thinking that her people did not avoid death; death was all around her in the village, especially in the winter, as the townspeople succumbed to illness, to accidents and to foolishness. Still, she didn't argue with the goblin; they just walked through the snow together.

Johanna's guild suffered from her absence during winter-festival preparations. With no strong voice to lead them, their pageant play for the festival suffered and died. For the first time in one hundred and eight years, their guild had no offering. A violent argument broke out at the winter guild meeting. Some said Johanna should be removed for instability and laziness, while others said her father's recent death meant she should be given leeway. Johanna heard all this second hand from Jack, but when she recounted it to the goblin, she did so without feeling, except for her description of the light that glinted off the metal buttons on Jack's overalls as he spoke to her. One had been polished while the other hadn't.

In the end, the guild left her in charge, but her assistant took over her duties. She felt only relief, since it gave her more time to walk in the forest with the goblin. Her outbursts about not going for walks were so severe that her family and friends had since stopped questioning her. Even on the day of winter festival, she left early in the morning to go out, and didn't return until well after the nighttime fires had died completely in their beds. Folks shook their heads, but the smell of roast goose and the promise of gifts quickly made them forget the fading girl.

Only her assistant, famed for his intuition that told him when cows were ill and when a surprise rain would come in quick and fast, had a hunch about what happened. "Never seen a goblin steal one of us before," Jack told his little sister, looking through the windows of their warm cottage out into the desolate snow. "But I don't see why we think it impossible." The girl shivered and drew closer to her brother, vowing never to be taken.

Spring

In the spring, Johanna and the goblin parted ways.

It started just as the first shoots of green began to show again. Johanna did not find the goblin at their usual meeting place. Certainly, he was only a few hundred feet away, looking at a fish in a nearby stream, but his absence chilled her; their unspoken contract meant that they *always* met in the same spot except in cases of emergency, and a fish in a stream was not Johanna's idea of an emergency. When she found the goblin she was out of sorts and felt irritated by his poking at the fish with a stick. "Leave the poor thing alone," she snapped, and he cringed, widening his yellow eyes at her. They walked sullenly and parted unhappy.

Johanna woke early in the morning, worried that she had offended the goblin, wondering if he would be there for her when she got up. What if he had disappeared or found something else to do? She started at the thought in terror. It had been so long since she'd spent the day any other way that not walking with the goblin filled her with dread. Yet when she arrived in the forest, he was there waiting for her with a gift, a small stone from the riverbed, rubbed smooth by the passing water. He'd just pulled it out before she'd arrived, and it lay in her palm, cold and dead against her skin.

The goblin grew more distracted, speaking to her less and wandering away from her to look at things in the forest. She now felt lonelier and more disconsolate than ever; she'd had one friend, and now even that friend would leave. The goblin developed an obsession with digging in the dirt, and would take an hour out of their walk to hack away at the thawing ground only to come up empty handed or, worse, emerge with a fistful of dirt that he treated as a treasure. Dirt caked his nails, and he would emit a strange, rotting smell. The blue beads, which the goblin had once heralded as his favorite possession now hung forgotten from the strap on his loincloth, growing scratched and grubby.

She came home at night and cried herself to sleep. Her mother and brother grew increasingly worried, but she couldn't think of where to begin to tell them what was wrong, and even when she told the tale to herself, she saw at once that she was unreasonable, strange, unhinged.

Finally, one day, the goblin simply wasn't there. Not at their usual spot, nor at any of the spots nearby. Johanna crashed through the forest, scaring birds and rabbits, but every patch of green she saw was just the promise of spring: the grass, shrubs, bushes, trees returning to life. She went home and sobbed uncontrollably, clutching at the stone the goblin had given her, which now grew warm in her hand.

Now that Johanna showed concrete, clear signs of distress, her family and friends rallied around her, bringing her gifts and sweet bread and flowers. Jack came to the house every day and gently sought to draw her by asking her advice on guild matters he'd already decided.

Her world flipped on its head. She absolutely refused to go out. At first she stared out of the windows obsessively toward the spot where she and the goblin would meet each day, barely listening to Jack as he talked of new storage buildings and accounts in arrears. When a dog would set the grass twitching, she'd jump, thinking she'd seen the goblin. She wondered if he thought of her.

Seeing her aversion to the outside world but not wanting to push her, Jack opened the window so that she could feel the spring breeze on her face. She turned away.

Slowly her spirit returned from the forest and settled in at the house, into her body. She began to offer Jack ideas about how to deal with those who had not settled their guild dues. While washing dishes in the spring sunshine, she listened to one of the designers of the new grain barn, who sat at the kitchen table. When he had finished his pitch, she agreed to buy two for the village's benefit if he made certain improvements to the design—and if he paid her in return for every time he used those improvements in future buildings. Even Jack admitted that it was a shrewd piece of bargaining, and he smiled approvingly at Johanna as he ushered the builder out of her house.

Finally she emerged from the house, too, and went to the guild hall to set things right. Everyone was pleased to see her; they seemed like new faces to her. They treated her gently but with respect, and within the week, everyone who had arrears had caught up on their payments.

Jack even sought out Johanna's advice about his little sister. Their mother had decided she should wed the son of the blacksmith in one of the other villages, but the girl had responded flatly. Johanna gave sensible advice about giving her time to think and react, and Jack's mother sent over a little yellow pepper plant in thanks.

Johanna still had violent twinges of longing for her days of rambling. The shade of the peppers, just the same as the goblin's eyes, could still bring her to tears in the early hours of the morning, but now she grew wily enough to make sure she slept through those hours. She'd find herself leaving the house meaning to go to town and inadvertently turn towards the forest, but she'd catch her steps and right herself again. Months passed and she didn't see the goblin.

As expected by everyone in the village, Jack asked Johanna to marry him, and as expected by everyone, she said yes. Over a long engagement, they began to plan a sensible wedding, but Johanna's time in the woods had changed her, and the details showed vague hints of melancholy: black on the table settings, little beads in the bottom of the flower vases that looked like the dead eyes of a crow. But Jack loved her and let her have her talismans.

In the last month of spring, Johanna emerged from her house and almost tripped on something that had been left on her front step. She bent down to goblin height and saw the little strand of blue beads. They were scratched and dirty, all shine gone from them, but when she rubbed them hard with her finger, she could still see the blue of the sky. She took them into her kitchen and cleaned them, each one, as the goblin had once cleaned them in a stream in the forest. As she did, she remembered him clearly and fondly. She cried as the water ran over her hands, but eventually her tears turned to laughter. Before she left her house, she put the bracelet around her wrist, both to render it harmless and to remind herself of what had transpired. When Jack saw it, he sighed with relief. "Gods," he said to himself. "He's returned what he stole."

She caught sight of the goblin a few times, but she remembered his trick from the early days and never looked directly at him again. If she saw him only out of the corner of her vision, she remained safe. She always knew him by his loping gait, and sometimes she felt indescribably pulled in his direction, but she kept her eyes firmly on the road and just kept moving.

Jack and Johanna's wedding passed smoothly, and towards the end of the spring, they moved into a small but beautiful house near the guild hall. Now they worried only about Jack's sister, whose life was planned from cradle to grave. She'd been disappearing into the woods for long hours. Jack paced up and down in front of the window. But Johanna was undisturbed. "She's got to come back on her own," she said to him softly, turning the scuffed blue beads around her wrist and touching each one in turn between her forefinger and thumb.

Skin

Kathleen Kelly

Quick! Close the door!" Stella giggled, shaking the rain out of her hair. Paul grinned mischievously at her as he pushed the door closed against the gusting wind. She wrapped her arms around his neck and planted a kiss on his cheek. "My hero," she said, tousling his dripping hair.

"Ugh, get a room. Can't you two wait until I'm not here?" Victoria drawled, popping a cigarette between her lips and preparing to light it.

"Hey! Not in here!" Stella gasped, moving to grab the cigarette. "My aunt will kill me if she smells smoke in here."

Victoria raised a sculpted eyebrow and pulled it out of her mouth. It was red where her lipstick had stained the end.

"Fine. Won't light anyway—it's too wet from the stupid rain."

Stella turned the light on to reveal the pristine interior of her aunt's old farmhouse. The light flickered as a particularly strong gust of wind hit the house.

"Great, we're gonna have a power outage. That'll be a real party killer."

"Come on, Vicky. Where's your sense of adventure?" Paul said with a wink.

"It'll arrive as soon as the booze does. Where's your brother at, anyway?" Victoria huffed, falling back onto the floral sofa.

"Harley said he'd be here just after eight." Stella replied, looking out the window. "He should be here soon, actually."

"He's still single, yeah? I could use a good distraction."

"Okay, firstly, eww! He's my twin brother. Find your distraction somewhere else. Secondly, what about Tom?"

"Tom hasn't talked to me in three days! I've texted him and called him and left him voicemails, and what does he do? Ignores me." Stella flipped her long black hair over her shoulder. "As far as I'm concerned, it's *so* over."

The door slammed open, banging against the wall.

"Damn wind!" Paul cursed, pushing it closed again. "Is it going to be doing that all night?"

"Just wait until Harley gets here, then we can lock it." Stella sat on the big leather armchair. The lights flickered again as a streak of lightning lit up the sky, and Paul counted until they heard the inevitable rumble of thunder.

"Twenty seconds. The storm's getting closer." Paul said.

"Are you sure the house isn't going to break apart? It's ancient," Victoria joked. Stella laughed.

"I'm sure. This house has been through everything imaginable."

The old farmhouse was one of Stella's favourite places. She and Harley had come here every summer to help her aunt and uncle. Victoria and Paul were from the neighboring town. Their families always came to Stella's aunt's annual cabaret. But Stella and her friends were too old to be hanging out with the kids there, and too young for the adults, so they'd decided to party their own way in the house.

"Hey, did you hear on the news about those killings?" Paul asked as he rejoined them in the living room.

"Yeah, two people skinned alive," Victoria said with a shudder. "Talk about the worst way to die."

"And they haven't even found the killer, according to my aunt," Stella chimed in. "She was so worried, she almost didn't go to the cabaret at all. And when she left, she kept telling me to lock all the doors and bar the windows, blah blah blah." She groaned. "It's like she doesn't trust me. Obviously I'm not going to let a killer in the house!"

The door slammed open again with a bang. Victoria screamed.

"Geeze, Victoria, you'd think someone was being murdered in here," Harley said from the doorway.

"It's not my fault! They were talking about murders and skinning people!"

Lightning flashed behind him as he walked in, illuminating the windblown trees in the farmyard. Paul counted again.

"Fifteen. It's definitely coming this way."

"Close the door, Harley—you're getting everything wet!" Stella shouted over the noise of the wind through the door. "And you're late. What took you so long?"

Harley walked into the house, dripping wet and grinning.

"My buddy is selling his gun for a great deal. Couldn't resist looking at it! I could use one to add to my hunting collection." He grinned at Stella as she rolled her eyes, and then held up two bottles of tequila. "Who's ready to party?"

"Thank God!" Victoria jumped off the couch and snagged one of the bottles, opening it and taking a swig. The wind buffeted against the door again. Lightning flashed across the sky, illuminating a figure standing in the road.

"Who is that?" Victoria said, squinting to see the stranger.

"I didn't see anyone when I came in," Harley replied, leaning slightly out the door.

"Somebody close the door," Stella whispered, discomforted. The stranger was standing oddly, head cocked awkwardly to the side. He stood rigidly, swaying occasionally with the storm.

"Turn on the light, I can't see."

"He hasn't seen us yet. Close the door!" Stella pushed through her friends to close it just as Victoria turned on the porch light, illuminating the figure's face.

"TOM!" she screeched. Stella couldn't tell by her voice whether Victoria was thrilled or furious. Stella clutched Victoria's arm as she struggled to run outside.

"Something's wrong, Vicky, wait!" Victoria lurched forward just as Tom collapsed onto the ground.

"He's hurt!" Victoria struggled free of Stella's grasp and ran down the driveway into the pouring rain. She dropped down beside Tom's prone form and called back at them, "Help me get him inside!"

Stella groaned inwardly as Harley and Paul ran outside. She felt unsettled. Lightning flashed again as the boys picked Tom up off the ground and began to head back toward the door. Stella shivered against the cold wind, wrapping her arms around herself. The boys came in carrying a very wet—and very dirty—Tom.

"Don't put him on the couch! He's filthy. Take him downstairs," Stella instructed, closing the door behind Victoria as she rushed in out of the downpour. She grabbed the old skeleton key off the hook and locked the door, then hung it up again. The locks were original; her aunt had never replaced them. Which explained why the doors couldn't stay shut against the wind without the locks anymore.

She sighed and hurried downstairs after her friends. She found them laying Tom down on the old green couch. Paul was checking his wrist for a pulse.

"No, you can't check a pulse with your thumb. Use your two fingers," Stella said as she walked closer. When she caught sight of Tom in the light, she gasped. He was pasty white, his lips almost blue and his filmy eyes were rolled back in his head. His once muscular body was now almost skeletal, and his clothing sagging from him like wet paper towel. He was completely covered in mud, but his skin was shiny and wet.

"Is he alive?" Victoria whispered, glancing from Tom to Paul and back again.

"There's no pulse," Paul murmured. He looked up at Stella, "We should call someone for help."

Stella pushed down the rising panic and nodded in agreement, pulling out her phone to call 911. Victoria began to cry, tears running black down her face as her makeup ran. Stella looked up from her phone, frowning.

"No service," she said.

"I'll try," Harley replied, hands shaking slightly as he pulled his phone from his pocket. "I don't have any service, either."

"Damn storm must have knocked out the lines," Paul muttered.

"You guys stay here, I'll drive to the cabaret and grab someone," Harley said, standing up. "I'll only be a few minutes."

"He can't be dead." Victoria said, anger flashing in her eyes. She turned on the corpse. "What, you think you can ignore me for three days and then die? I hate you!" She screamed, slapping Tom's face with a resounding smack. As she pulled her hand away, the skin from Tom's face stuck, pulling off in strands and revealing the bone underneath. Victoria shrieked, standing quickly and shaking her hand frantically, trying to dislodge the sticky skin. Harley cursed and backed toward the stairs while Paul puked onto the floor. Stella watched in morbid fascination as Tom's body lurched forward, his hand grabbing Victoria's wrist. She screamed as the skin pulled itself off of his body, sliding to the floor in a thick, amorphous mass. Tendrils of the milky-clear substance reached toward Victoria as Tom's now skinless body crumpled to the ground.

"Oh my God, oh my God," Paul kept muttering, his eyes wide as globes. The skin wrapped around Victoria's ankles as she struggled to free herself from its sticky grasp. She looked at them, fear in her eyes, as it quickly climbed her body, reaching her neck.

"Help," she whispered, and screamed again as it covered her face, forcing its way into her nose and eyes. Her body convulsed, then became still, her skin slick and shiny as Tom's had been. A low groan escaped her pale, slimy lips as the last of the mass slid over them and into her open mouth. She was motionless, staring blankly up at the ceiling, completely enveloped by the seemingly alive blob that was now melding into her skin. Slowly, she turned her head toward them, taking a step forward. Her eyes were milky white, covered by the now thin film of the creature. She reached out a hand toward them.

They ran.

They stumbled over each other up the stairs to the main floor and slammed the door behind them.

"Block it!" Stella gasped, backed up against the wall. Harley grabbed a chair from the kitchen and shoved it under the door handle. Paul stood bent over, panting.

"We need to get out of here," Stella gasped as they heard a dull thud from the basement.

"I think it's trying to climb the stairs," Harley said. Another thud resounded from behind the door, closer this time. Paul backed up into the wall, panic-stricken.

"It's g-going to k-kill us, j-just like Tom, j-just like Victoria," he stammered, running his shaking hands through his still damp hair.

"No, it's not," Harley said. "I've got an idea."

"If your idea is that we get out of here, I'm in," Paul said, heading towards the door. Harley winked and bounded up the stairs.

"No!" Stella cried. "We have to save Victoria! We can't just abandon her."

Thump. Thump.

It had reached the door. White, slimy fingers slid underneath, clutching at the floorboards.

"Listen to me!" Paul held her hands in his. His eyes were bloodshot and sweat dripped down his forehead. "Stella, we can't save her. Did you see that thing? Did you? It's a monster. That—thing—wasn't acting like Victoria! It doesn't even look like her. If we go near it it's going to get us just like it did her!" He was trembling, and his hands were slick enough that she could pull away from his vice-like grip.

"No, you're wrong!"

"He ain't wrong, Stella." Harley stepped down the last stair, holding a shotgun from his collection. "We've got to put an end to this now. Victoria isn't Victoria anymore." He aimed the gun at the bottom of the door where Victoria's fingers were still grasping at the floorboards. The skin didn't seem fully attached, and stuck like Silly Putty to the floor as the fingers stretched toward them.

"No!" Stella screamed, and Paul held her back as Harley fired round after round into the door. The fingers stopped moving. Blood began to seep under the door.

"You've killed her!" Stella shrieked, trying to pull away from Paul's grip. "How could you?"

"It had to be done. I'm sorry." Harley set the gun against the wall and took her from Paul, hugging her close. "She wasn't human anymore, don't you see?"

"Let's get out of here," Paul interrupted, walking once more to the door. "We have to get to the cabaret and warn everyone. Get help."

Stella nodded. Numb, she let Harley guide her to the entrance. Paul stepped aside as she got the key off the hook and moved to unlock the door. Her hands shook as she tried to fit the key into the keyhole. She took a deep breath, trying to calm herself.

"Ah!" Paul shrieked. Harley and Stella turned around to see the skin oozing from under the door. It had grabbed Paul's ankle and proceeded to slink slowly up his leg. "No!" He frantically tried to wipe it off with his hands, only to end up with them covered in it as it slowly enveloped his body.

"Paul!" Stella cried, reaching a hand out toward him.

"Stella, unlock the door! Quickly!" Harley yanked the key out of her hand, only to drop it to the floor. It clanked against the hardwood and bounced straight into the register on the floor. They shared a glance.

"Run," Harley whispered. Stella spared one look at Paul as he began to shudder violently, the sliminess of the parasite slowly dissipating into his skin, leaving a thin, shiny film. She dashed past him on one side, Harley on the other, and he grabbed her hand and dragged her up the stairs and into his room. He shut the door behind him and locked it.

"Where are we going? We should have gone to the back door!"

"We can't leave it to roam around! We've got to find a way to kill it!"

"No, we have to find a way to save Paul!" Tears ran freely down Stella's face as she held back a sob. "This is insane. What is happening?" She clutched him, eyes wide.

"I don't know. It seems to need a host, though, so killing Paul is the only way to stop it." They heard a thump as it forced Paul's body up the stairs.

"You can't!" she cried, and he put a hand over her mouth, smothering her.

"Shh!" he hissed. "We don't know if it can hear us!" She relaxed and he let her go.

"Can we get out your window?" she asked, surveying the small room.

"It's too high."

"We could tie your sheets . . . " she trailed off as another thump sounded, closer to the door.

"It's eventually going to find its way in here, Stella," Harley whispered, looking around. "I've got my other shotgun in here. You can shoot it, right?"

She shook her head, shaking at the thought.

"I can't shoot Paul," she said, wiping her runny nose on her sleeve.

"I can't leave you defenseless. You're my sister, Stella. I'm supposed to protect you." He got up and rummaged through his closet, coming out with another shotgun and an axe. Stella raised her eyebrow. He shrugged.

"I needed them for hunting."

"*Need* is a strong word," she muttered, and they shared a nervous laugh. Another thump came again, right in front of the door.

"Quick, Stella, tie the sheets. I'll load the gun." The doorknob rattled, and another strong thump sounded against the wood. Stella frantically ripped the sheets off Harley's bed and tied them to the bedpost. She forced the window open and threw the sheets outside, watching them unravel toward the ground.

"It's not long enough!" she said frantically, looking down. The wind blasted into her, pushing her back into the room and soaking her with rain.

"It'll have to be," Harley replied slowly, staring at the door. "It's figured out how to turn a doorknob." He handed the loaded gun to her, and she once again shook her head.

"I can't, Harley."

He sighed and handed her the axe.

"At least take this, then." She clutched tightly at the weapon, fear clawing at her insides. Her heart pounded in her ears as the door slowly opened.

Lightning flashed, illuminating Paul's ghostly pale features. His skin was shiny and white, and his face was devoid of expression. His blank eyes stared forward, not quite focused. He cocked his head, as if counting the seconds. It was all the time Harley needed.

He shot at Paul. The skin around the wound hissed and retracted, slowly peeling off the dying body. Paul coughed, blood oozing out of his mouth and splattering across the floor. His chest oozed blood onto his shirt, the colour spreading outward as it drenched the fabric.

"Come on, Stella, let's go!" Harley yelled, running toward her and the window. He made it to the end of the bed when a slick hand came down on his shoulder. The parasite slid from Paul's body to Harley's and wrapped him up in itself, tendril upon tendril of thick, slimy, skin-like substance frantically climbing over his body. Paul fell to the ground, blood staining the floor, his eyes open even in death.

"Kill me," Harley croaked as the skin wormed its way into his mouth. His eyes were wide with horror. "Do it!"

"No!" Stella sobbed, backing toward the window, tears pouring from her eyes. She watched in horror as Harley's body became stiff, his features contorted. He took one step forward, then another, his movements stiff and jarring. She backed up until she was pressed against the wall, axe clutched in front of her. Finally, in front of her, his arm reached out, slick white fingers outstretched. His hand closed around her arm and she screamed as she felt the rubbery texture of the parasite on her skin. Instinctively she pushed forward with all her strength, panic rising in her chest. Harley stumbled backward and she slashed at him with the axe. He staggered; skin bubbling as the parasite tried to keep him upright. His eyes clouded over as his blood dripped onto the carpet, and the skin pulled off him, shuddering as if agitated. It didn't have eyes, it was just an amorphous mass, but Stella could feel its attention on her in the way her skin crawled. It reared up like a cobra, poised to strike. She turned toward the window and jumped, propelling herself over the edge and clutching for the sheet rope as it lunged for her.

She was lying on the ground in front of the house when her aunt arrived.

"Stella!" her aunt cried, running over and crouching down beside her. "What happened? You look like death!"

Stella tried to scream, but no sound came out.

The Night Parade of Hiro Doji

Aimee Picchi

The Supreme Commander rapped his folded fan across my horns, right on the place where they were the most sensitive. I was washing up from lunch and hadn't heard the *nurihyon* sneak up behind me.

"Hiro Doji, listen up," he told me. "You have a very important job for this year's Night Parade."

"Oh?" My ears twitched. My parade job had always been the least important of any *yokai* in Tokyo. I swept up after the demons, removing all traces of the humans who caught a forbidden glimpse of the annual festival.

"The Lady Kitsune of Kyoto has decided to join us," the Commander said, his wrinkled head nodding like a dried gourd swinging in an autumn wind. "This is a great honor for the *yokai* of Tokyo, and we must show her all due respect."

I continued drying the teapot, wondering what role I would have. Clean her room? Scout out a fine gift from the Ginza department stores?

My puzzled look made the Commander laugh. "Don't work that demon brain too hard, Hiro Doji, or you might fry it like a piece of tofu. I need you to watch her youngest daughter. It's the first time the girl has been in the city, and I need you to make sure she doesn't get into any trouble."

"You want me to babysit?"

The Commander chuckled and patted my arm. "That's what I love about *oni*. Like pigs, you dig at the roots."

Since I had only met one of my kind, my late mother, I had to take the Commander's word for what we *oni* were like. Seven decades ago, Mother died protecting her treasures and me when soldiers attacked our mountain cave. While I survived, the alabaster box holding our two sacred relics, the mallet of wishes and the coat of invisibility, vanished. The Supreme Commander had promised to help me find them if I first served him for a century.

The swish of his lush silk robes signaled the old demon's departure. I called after him, "But who will clean up after the parade, sir?"

The Commander's eyebrows furrowed. "Surely you can do that, as well?"

I placed the teapot next to the sink, imagining carrying a toddler fox-girl on my shoulders while attending my other duties. "That will be difficult, Commander."

He sighed. "Fine, Hiro Doji. You don't have much longer until you've repaid me. Only thirty more years of servitude." He gave me a magnanimous smile. "For a bonus, I'll shave off one day from your debt."

Lady Kitsune arrived with an entourage of ten fox maidens. They pranced on dainty white feet and wore kimonos cut down to their small shapes. The lady, though, appeared entirely human, without a trace of whiskers or tails. Only the most powerful *kitsune* could hide their fox shapes like that.

"Morimoto-san," the lady said, smiling down on my boss, who, standing as tall as he could, only came up to her bust. "How charming your home is. And how lucky we are to be your guests in Tokyo."

Morimoto? I never knew the Commander had a name, and what a common one at that.

The Commander waved in my direction. "This is Hiro Doji, the *oni*. He'll watch your daughter during the Night Parade."

The lady gave me a slight bow.

"Do not let my daughter near any human males, *oni*," she said. "They don't agree with her constitution."

She and the Commander continued on their tour of the suburban house, which belonged to a wealthy human family but was "borrowed" for this year's celebration. During my seven decades of employment, we had usurped hundreds of human homes, with the Supreme Commander using his *nurihyon* mind tricks to kick out their residents.

Because the Commander resembled nothing more than an old man, he was the first of us to mainstream into modern society. All *yokai* looked up to him.

A shriek caught my attention, followed by the clattering of heels.

A teenaged girl burst into the room, teetering on stilettos. Her hair was dyed a rainbow of colors—pink, orange, blue, purple and green—and teased into a bouffant at the back, pinned with several sizes of bright bows. Her clothes matched the color scheme, and dozens of rings, bracelets and necklaces chimed in. Her eyebrows had been plucked off her face, and repainted as tiny commas. Green eye shadow blossomed at the corners of her large black eyes, which narrowed as she caught sight of me.

I took a step away from her. This certainly wasn't a toddler *kitsune*.

"This is some sort of joke, right? My mom expects me to stay out in the boonies?" she said. "And you! My mom said an *oni* would show me around the city." She gave me a scornful look. "If you're an *oni*, where are your fangs?"

She poked at my lips, trying to look inside my mouth.

I growled. She snatched her fingers back.

"The Commander convinced a dentist to shave down my teeth," I said, remembering how he told me it was necessary to fit into city life. "But I can still tear off a human head in one bite."

The girl smiled and stuck out her hand. "That's more like it, Mr. Demon. I'm Hana." She sat down on the arm of a chair. "So, what are we going to do for fun before this stupid freak parade?"

As soon as the taxi pulled up to the front of the zoo, Hana groaned.

"No way," she said. "I live with a pack of foxes. I'm not spending another minute around animals."

"Have you seen a polar bear?" I said. "On my day off, I come here to watch him. He usually sits like this—" I placed my head on my hand "—and stares into space. I think he misses the North Pole."

"Any other ideas?" she said, as she clambered out of the car.

"How about visiting Tokyo's largest Gundam store? It's just a few streets over there," I pointed.

"You mean, like, toy models? The kinds that little human boys play with?" Her eyebrows furrowed, forming sharp thorns.

"And grown men and . . . and sometimes demons," I said, shuffling my feet and feeling silly at my attempts to entertain this young *yokai*, who was about the age I was when my mother died.

Hana laughed, the sound of water rushing through a mountain stream, and took off in the direction of the Gundam store.

"Wait!" I yelled. She disappeared into the crowd, and I cursed. *"Kuso!"*

Leaning my head back, I inhaled, getting the scent of Hana's perfume into my nose, and ignoring the scents of the city, diesel engines and unwashed humans. I hadn't tracked since I left the mountains, and it made me feel young and wild again.

When I glanced around, the plate-glass window of the zoo gave me a start. In it was reflected a fat creature with skin that appeared sunburned, hair gelled up to cover the tips of his horns, looking ready to blow steam from his ears.

In short, an overweight *oni* with a bad hairstyle.

Hana's perfume led right to the Gundam store. What on earth had prompted her to take off so quickly?

I pushed my way through the crowds. Families, kids and men in their twenties and thirties crowded the shop, but there was no sign of the rainbow-haired girl on any of its five levels. Finally, I asked a clerk if she had passed through, describing Hana's hair and clothing.

"Maybe," he shrugged, but his eyes laughed at me. "What's an oaf like you want with someone like that, anyway?"

My mother hadn't prepared me to live with humans, with their little lies and big ones, their envy and their thieving. I grabbed the clerk's neck with my hand and asked again, less politely. He gave another noncommittal answer and I pushed him away so hard that he hit a shelf of models, setting off a cascade of clinking plastic toys.

My mother would have torn the clerk apart. "We feed on the secrets that hide within humans' hearts," she told me once, stirring her stew pot. "From their bones, you grow into a mighty *oni*. Only a strong stick can break a false bell."

But a modern *oni* can't go around ripping into humans.

Just then, I caught Hana's perfume again. It took me up a set of utility stairs and onto the roof.

The setting sun cast long shadows across the gravel underfoot. Hana leaned against an air-conditioning unit, a man slumped at her side. Her eyes were glowing, the color of molten lava, and sharp little fox teeth smiled at me.

"Mr. Demon!" she called. "I caught a human for you to eat."

I picked up the man, who hung limply from my arms. "What did you do to him?"

"Don't worry. You can have the leftovers. I just sucked out his life's essence. Yummy," she said, licking her lips with a delicate tongue.

"What?" *Kitsune* liked to play tricks on humans, but sucking out a human's *ki?* That seemed, well, barbaric.

"Dummy, I'm a dark *kitsune*, not one of those silly fox ladies who drink tea," she said. "You told me this store would have human men, and wow! You were so right. Now I'm juiced! Let's go!" She took a step, but her eyes widened in panic as she wobbled and leaned toward me, like a ship about to sink. She moaned and put a hand to her forehead. "I think that guy over-amped me. I'm not feeling very good, Mr. Demon."

Then she threw up on my shoes.

Darkness settled over Tokyo like a superhero's cape. I slung Hana over my shoulder and stepped onto the roof's parapet. I might be fat and fangless, but I still had the strength to jump across buildings.

Or at least, that was my hope. We needed to get away before some employees discovered Hana's victim.

I closed my eyes and counted to three, then launched myself into the air between the buildings. Once, such a leap would have been like a child's hop across a stream, but now my biggest physical work-out was hauling the groceries. To my relief, my feet met the floor of the building across the street with a solid thud.

Confidence bolstered, I made several more jumps, until I could see the dark expanse of Ueno Park, adorned with a necklace of delicate lamplight.

Hana groaned and opened her green-rimmed eyes. The red glow of her pupils had faded to an ember.

"Mr. Demon," she said, heaving. I leaned her over my knee so that she wouldn't throw up on me again. "Should've listened to my mother. Said I wasn't ready." She rubbed her eyes, smudging her makeup. "Please don't tell her. If my sisters find out, they'll never let me forget. Every family meal, one of them will bring this up. I hate older sisters. I'll do anything, just don't tell on me."

"Hmm," I said. The Supreme Commander might not give me my bonus if he learned I hadn't obeyed the Lady Kitsune's instructions. I had to decide whether I could swallow an untruth for the sake of one day shaved from my debt.

Hana patted my arm. "You're not what I expected from an *oni.*"

"What do you mean?"

She gave me an odd look, but didn't answer.

"There must be some *oni* living around Kyoto," I prodded.

Hana shook her head. "There used to be a lair in the Kitayama mountains, but all the *oni* were killed by Japanese soldiers a long time ago. The Supreme Commander told my mother the story one night. I was hiding behind a screen and overheard. He said he just happened to be close to their lair when the soldiers attacked. By the time he got there, all the *oni* were dead."

"My mother was killed by Japanese soldiers, too. And the Supreme Commander also was close by, but he helped me fight off the attackers," I said.

"No offense, but is that why you're his lapdog? *Oni* are supposed to be fierce and wild."

I growled. "He saved my life, although he arrived too late for my mother," I said, turning away from her, so she wouldn't see the tears that sprang to my eyes. "But when the battle was over, my mother's treasures were missing, and he vowed to track them down if I gave him one hundred years of service."

Hana laughed scornfully. "A century, and for what? Some cave trinkets? Animal hides?"

"My mother sometimes delivered fortune upon the deserving." She had two sides, bright and dark, frightening and generous. She was like a storm, most often bringing destruction, but occasionally—and it was as rare as stars on a cloudy night—also a fresh start.

She grabbed my arm. "The mallet of wishes and the coat of invisibility?"

"You've heard of them?" I widened my eyes in surprise.

"You're freaking kidding me! They're legendary!" She jumped up and did a little dance. "What are you waiting for, you big lump! We've got to find them—like, tonight!"

Sighing, I stood up and brushed the building's rooftop gravel from my pants. "I tried, Hana. I tried for years after my mother's death. Eventually, I agreed to the Supreme Commander's deal."

"You're dumber than you look, you know that?" Hana said. "I've got a better deal for you—if you promise to keep my, um, accident a secret, I'll help you find your treasures."

"How could you know where they are?"

Hana frowned and tapped her foot. "Deal or no deal?"

"Deal," I sighed.

"That little sneak has your treasures," she said.

I looked at her blankly. "What sneak?"

She grabbed my arms and yelled, "The Supreme Commander! I never liked that *yokai*, always lording it over the rest of us."

"I don't think so, Hana," I said, shaking my head. "Why would he do that?"

"Why does he kick humans out of their own homes? Why does he insist we call him Supreme Commander? Why does a snake slither in the grass?" she said.

Could it be? Could he have stolen the treasures while my mother and I were fighting the soldiers? It seemed unlikely, and even more so given that I had lived with him for seventy years and never seen a glimpse of the alabaster box.

"That's crazy," I said, forcing an awkward laugh from my belly. "I would have seen the treasures by now if he had them."

She thought for a minute. "That's because they're hidden at his house."

I scoffed, "The Supreme Commander doesn't have a home."

Hana tapped her nose. "That shows how little you know. I also overheard him telling my mother he has a secret home here in Tokyo."

A *kitsune's* sense of smell is even keener than an *oni's*, and a teenaged fox-girl is fleeter than an overweight demon. I huffed and puffed as I kept pace with Hana as she raced past trinket shops selling bamboo plants and rice crackers, twisted through dark alleys, stopped at dead-ends and backtracked along an old temple's walls.

After hours of racing through the streets of Tokyo, Hana led us to a narrow street in the heart of the Asakusa neighborhood, one that I had never noticed before. A dark energy tingled my fingers as we walked by a stone wall. Curious, I touched it and jumped back as a shock traveled through my arm: a phantom wall.

I pushed my way through the illusory barrier, pain coursing through my body and making my horns ache, and broke down the door behind it. Hana popped in after me, rubbing her arms to disperse the charge.

The scene before us was crazy, a tiny studio apartment packed with stuff: a *biwas, shamisens,* jewels and parchments, heaped from floor to ceiling. And, on top of the biggest pile, my mother's alabaster box.

What kind of a person would hoard treasures like this? And how could he have tricked me into a century of servitude, all while smiling to my face? My heart raced and anger coursed through my body.

I had given decades to the worst of the worst, a *yokai* who would lie to his own kind. My hands clenched into fists.

Before we had time to breathe, a wisp of white smoke twirled around us and took shape as a comely young woman. A white kimono clung to her graceful form, and her long, dark hair was twisted into a bun. She smiled at me with a rosebud mouth, but I remained stone-faced. She could be a ghost, haunting one of the stolen treasures.

When she leaned toward Hana, a second face at the back of her head leered at me with sharp teeth. This was no ghost, but a two-faced demon, set to guard the Supreme Commander's hoard.

"Watch out, Hana!" I yelled.

The demon's hair unraveled into snake-line vines, reaching out for the *kitsune* and wrapping the girl's hands as if in duct tape. I got in a few good kicks, until the two-faced monster's hair whipped toward my feet and tripped me up.

The handle of a katana stuck out from a pile of loot. As I reached for it, the two-faced demon's hair coiled around my right hand and gave me a yank, pulling me from the weapon.

Hana clasped her bound hands together. Murmuring words under her breath, a glowing orb formed between her hands.

Fox fire!

As the orb released from her hands, it picked up speed and hurtled toward the demon's face. The creature screamed and ducked, and her hair loosened.

I grabbed the katana with a roar, lunging and taking off the two-faced demon's head with one blow. The demon continued gnashing its teeth as it hit the floor, moaning, "I'm so hungry."

"Eat steel, hag!" Hana yelled at her.

The Night Parade was a wild tour through Tokyo's dark streets, set to clanging and thrumming music.

First, the *chochin-obake,* lighting the way with their bulging eyes and lantern bellies. Twanging notes sang from strings of the *shami-choro,* its long legs folding inward like a duck's, while the crockery general pounded his stomach with old spoons.

Then the slit-faced women, the faceless monks, the lumps of living flesh that smelled like rotting meat, with the *tanukis* playing their round bellies like drums. The *kappas* crept along while the nightmare-eating *baku* peered into dark bedrooms. Hana's mom and her *kitsune* maidens made a lovely host of fleet-footed creatures. And in the midst of it all, the Supreme Commander, his huge, wrinkled head bobbing serenely, lifted on a palanquin carried by four giant earth-spiders.

Hana nudged me in the ribs.

I put on the coat of invisibility, so old and worn it felt as brittle as dried rice noodles.

I walked through the parade like a fish swimming upstream. If other *yokai* bumped against me, they took no notice.

When I reached the Supreme Commander, I clambered on his palanquin, causing it to tilt to one side.

"Who's there?" he gasped.

Taking off the coat, I revealed myself. "Your humble servant."

The Supreme Commander paled as he looked at the coat.

"I had your best interest at heart, Hiro Doji. You were feral, a mountain savage living in a cave," he said. The earth spiders continued to move, unable to see us above them, but some of the *yokai* had taken notice of me. "Your mother was worse, an *oni* set in her ways. But in you, I saw potential."

I narrowed my eyes. "It's hard to believe a snake when it proclaims to tell the truth."

I took out the mallet of wishes and struck it against the palanquin, causing it to chime a golden tone. I whispered my desires into the ringing sound: first, that the Supreme Commander would proclaim his lies to the Night Parade.

As he yelled into the night, drawing the creatures' attention, spilling his guts about stealing the treasures of all the *yokai*, the Night Parade turned on him, all the fur, fangs and claws of Tokyo's beasts pulling him from the palanquin. At the side of the mob, I caught sight of Hana with a vulpine grin. *"Yatta!"* she yelled above the frenzy. We did it, indeed. I grinned at her.

But there was more to my wish.

The *yokai* left the Supreme Commander alive.

The old demon faced a long night as the parade's one-*yokai* cleanup crew.

And when that was done, he would repay his crimes with one thousand years of servitude to Tokyo's only *oni*.

Interview with Rin Chupeco
Author of *The Girl From the Well*

How would you describe The Girl from the Well *in three words?*

Creepy, subversive,—and sad.

When did you first have the idea to write a story inspired by the legend of Okiku?

I used to work at an office situated inside one of the oldest buildings in the city. The lights flickered often, and everything was old and rickety—stairs, doors, floors, elevators. It was a job that required a lot of overtime, so I often found myself clocking out late at night. Unfortunately, there were also other people working late in other floors below mine. Even more unfortunately, I had long hair, pale skin, and liked wearing dark clothes. I've also been frequently told I look Japanese or Korean, rather than look the Chinese girl that I was.

So, imagine having to work late, waiting for the rickety elevator to get to your floor while lights flickered in and out overhead, and then watching the doors slide open only to find me waiting inside.

A couple of those guys I'd inadvertently victimized could really hit those high notes. I nearly gave one Japanese man a heart attack – apparently I resembled an acquaintance of his who had died a few years ago.

I didn't mind being mistaken for a ghost, because people have done that since I was eight. The book's inspiration came about though, after everyone finally got used to me and started calling me 'the friendly building ghost'. "Sadako" was actually their pet name for me. The idea of a scary but inherently good ghost gained momentum after that.

A number of the scenes in this book are quite gruesome. Did you find them difficult to write?

They were very easy to write, and I'm not sure what that says about me. I grew up reading scary novels and wasn't really afraid of ghosts as a child—documentaries and horror movies were my bedtime fare, and I was relatively nightmare-free for most of my childhood. Stephen King and Peter Straub were early inspirations, so I've been writing stories about people's heads getting lopped off or about things under the bed long before I considered writing as a career I could take. I found the quieter moments where Okiku chooses not to kill more difficult to write about, because profundity for me is always harder to convey.

Are there any other folktales you would like to tackle in the future?

One WIP I'm currently working on uses mythical animals as a theme, with a strong focus on (though not limited to) Philippine mythology, which is so unique and diverse that I'm surprised few people have written about it yet. We're talking about fetus-eating women who can separate their waist and legs from their upper body, reverse centaurs, headless monsters who like wearing underwear on their heads, and more.

Another WIP that I've completed has a firebird as a central theme to a plot that's very fairy-tale-centric and with an ensemble cast. It's a low fantasy that's equal parts action and comedy, but needs a few more revisions before I'll be satisfied with it.

This novel has a very unique, poetic structure. Did you plan to write the novel this way? Or did it happen once you got into the story?

Okiku's character is the sole reason for the poetic structure—had I written the book based on anyone else's point of view, it would have sounded very different (a sequel to *The Girl from the Well*, based on another character's point of view, is written using more conventional means, since this protagonist is more grounded in reality than she is). I wanted the book to be the canvas she could paint herself as, using her quirks and traits as brushstrokes. I wanted the novel to sound vague and aimless at times (excepting the main plot points) the way a ghost might sound when she's telling her story, which is why it sometimes drifts or breaks off at the same time her mind wanders.

Do you have any advice for aspiring horror writers?

Write in the way the concept of horror speaks to you. If horror to you is a dripping gorefest of blood and bodies, then write that. If horror to you is a fade-to-black intimation, where the debauchery happens behind the scenes because the imagination makes this scarier, then write that. If horror to you is a sad story, about the redemption of things that are conventionally denied redemption (like it is to me), then write that, too.

Since the theme of this issue is monsters tell us . . . What monster do you consider the scariest?

Would it be so cliched to say that I think people at their worst is the scariest monster anyone could ever think of? Because I read about ghosts and monsters and watch them in movies, and can still understand their motivations, even if misguided—but then I go and read the news, or look outside, and I realize there's no monster so disturbing as the ones you have to live with.

I will say though, that whoever created the *kuchisake-onna*/slit-mouthed ghost is a very mentally sick human being who needs a lot of therapy, and I will love them forever for it.

Your favourite monster movie?

Ju-On: The Grudge series. *The Grudge,* which is its American remake, has its own twisted charm, but nothing beats the original Japanese movies for being the absurd body horror/psychological trauma triggers that I always love and look for in my scary movies.

The best book you've read recently?

I am also a very avid crime junkie (I suppose ghosts and serial killers go hand in hand) and I just recently got my hands on an English translation of *She Lover of Death,* one of the Erast Fandorin mysteries by Boris Akunin. I LOVE this series.

Rin Chupeco has always maintained her sense of humor despite uncanny resemblances to Japanese revenants,. Raised in Manila, Philippines, she keeps four pets: a dog, two birds, and a husband. She's been a technical writer and travel blogger, but now makes things up for a living. *The Girl from the Well* is her debut novel. Connect with Rin at www.rinchupeco.com

Interview with Hillary Monahan
Author of *Mary: The Summoning*

Describe *MARY: The Summoning* in three words for our readers.

Poor life choices.

(Seriously? Creepy, crawly, suspenseful.)

What gave you the idea to write about Bloody Mary? Did you play this game as a child?

Well, I said I played it but was actually lying through my teeth, so does that count? My hometown didn't have Bloody Mary as most folks know it. We had Mary Jane. According to local legend, when the Howard School in West Bridgewater burned to the ground in the fifties, Mary Jane got trapped in the bathroom and died in the school. If you went into any of the bathrooms in the NEW school and said her name three times with the lights out, Mary Jane would appear and scratch off your face. Also, four matching anything (Twinkies, rocks, ketchup packets) meant Mary Jane was close and wanted your blood.

So did I go into the bathroom and shut off the lights? You bet. Did I come screaming out of the bathroom? Yep! Did I actually say the name in the dark? NOPE.

Some of your descriptions of Mary during the summoning, really brought out the creepiness of the story. Was it difficult to get into the horror mindset while writing?

Not really but only because horror is a part of my household. No, I don't mean I'm married to a serial killer (I don't think) but more that my husband is a HUGE fan and we have hundreds upon hundreds of horror DVDs and books. From *Coffin Joe* to *Evil Dead* to *The Orphanage*, we have it in house. Anytime I needed a dose of tingly to get me in the right mindset, I visit my husband's collection and find myself a scare.

Do you have a group of friends like the girls in MARY: The Summoning?

I did in high school, though most of my friends now are male gamers who rage at internet dragons for fun. I can't say the cast is necessarily based on anyone I knew, but I suppose the girls represent archetypes in any social stratosphere: the leader (Jess), the sidekick (Shauna), the brain (Anna), the introvert (Kitty.)

Are you planning on taking on any other ghost stories in the future?

Oh, yes. I have a soft spot for ghosts because, of all the monsters, they scare me the most. I can behead a zombie, stake a vampire, or put a silver bullet in a werewolf. What do I do to a ghost? Yell obscenities at it until it cries?

Do you have any advice for aspiring horror writers? Is there a trick to writing those scary scenes?

Pacing, pacing, pacing. Absolutely necessary for horror to work. Make sure you mete out your scenes with enough downtime in between that the reader can recover, but without so much downtime that they get bored. Also, remember that horror is more than just visual. Describing what a scary thing looks like helps get the reader into your headspace, but giving them the smells, the sounds, the feel of things . . . that's what makes a monster fire on all cylinders. It puts flesh on the bones.

Since the theme of this issue is monsters tell us . . . What monster do you consider the scariest?

I'm the most terrible terrible that ever terribled. I already answered. Beyond ghosts, though, I will NOPE right out of alien stuff, too. I've never been able to sit through the movie *Alien* or *Close Encounters*. This started with a childhood trauma involving ET that I won't get into because we don't have all year.

You favourite monster movie?

Either *The Orphanage* or *The Ring*. Or maybe *Behind the Mask: The Rise of Leslie Vernon*.

The best book you've read recently?

The Girl With All the Gifts by M R Carey.

Hillary Monahan is Eva Darrows is also an international woman of mystery. Holed up in Massachusetts with three smelly basset hounds, she writes funny, creepy things for fun and profit.

Book Reviews

Servants of the Storm by Delilah S Dawson

When Hurricane Josephine blows through Savannah, Georgia, it changes everything. Homes and businesses are destroyed, and Dovey's best friend, Carly, was swept away. Unable to cope, Dovey suffered a psychotic break, and she has been living in a medicated stupor ever since. But one day she decides she doesn't want to feel fuzzy anymore, and she's going to stop taking the pills, no matter what the consequences may be. She never expected that the truth the pills were hiding from her would be so sinister.

Simon Pulse,
August 5, 2014

Carly isn't dead . . . at least Dovey doesn't think she is, after seeing her one day in their favourite cafe. As she begins searching for her friend in earnest, she finds there are many more secrets hiding in the shadows of Savannah. But there's no turning back for her now.

Dovey is an interesting character—you will spend a fair portion of the novel wondering if you can even trust her narration. After her breakdown she is placed on anti-psychotic medication, which she then stops taking without telling her doctor. So when she begins to see her dead friend, as well as demons, throughout the city, you want to believe her but are unsure whether or not you can. Even now having finished the book I wonder how much of it was true and how much she may have hallucinated. I'm personally a big fan of the unreliable narrator because it keeps you on your toes while reading.

What Dovey finds hiding in the shadows of Savannah is pandemonium a.k.a. all the demons. They've gathered there to feed off human despair and misery, and are collecting servants in their wake. It's soon obvious to her that she can't fight them alone and she enlists the help of her other childhood best friend, Baker, and a mysterious, handsome boy, named Isaac, who is clearly hiding something. I liked all of these characters—they were all unique, and they brought their own sets of skills and experiences to the table. Isaac is a particularly compelling character, because, like Dovey, his character is unreliable and you can never be sure where his allegiance lies. I was a little disappointed, however, when their team-up became more of a love triangle. The best friend versus the handsome, beguiling stranger is an overused trope and one that I could have done without. Thankfully this plot line stuck to the sidelines and didn't detract too much from the main story.

Servants of the Storm is a deeply haunting and atmospheric read. Dawson beautifully articulates the feel of the Deep South, post-hurricane. The entire book is quite evocative, and feels damp, dark and dangerous. It was clear to me that she is no stranger to writing more disturbing, sometimes graphic content, and that she has significant experience writing in this genre/style. If you favour darker paranormal/supernatural stories, you will find yourself at home within the pages of this book. You are in good hands.

—Christa Seeley

GHOST
HOUSE

ALEXANDRA
ADORNETTO
NEW YORK TIMES bestselling author of the HALO Trilogy

Harlequin Teen,
August 26, 2014

Ghost House by Alexandra Adornetto

Ghost House is an interesting take on your classic ghost story. The book opens up with Chloe already being able to see ghosts, but the situation gets worse when Chloe relocates to her grandmother's house in England. After the move she is truly haunted by ghosts that previously lived there.

The biggest difficulty I had while reading this story was the pacing. It takes a bit of time and energy to really get into everything that is happening, and I found my attention sometimes drifting. But in the end, the book does have a lot of great qualities that will creep some readers out—especially if you believe in ghosts.

What I really did enjoy about *Ghost House,* was the relationship Chloe had with her family. Particularly, the way Chloe acted with them, especially her brother. You could also tell that she had a special relationship with her mother before she died, there are a lot of mentions of how she wishes she could still talk to her mom. The love interest turned me off a bit, it came up too quickly and seemed a bit forced. But let's get back to the ghosts, which is what got me to continue with the story even through the tough parts.

After arriving at her grandmother's house in England, Chloe begins to be haunted by ghosts, and there is a mystery behind why these two, Alex and Isobel, are still at the house. Not only can Chloe communicate with them, but she begins to travel back into the past and see how their relationship with one another developed. In a way, this was an interesting addition to the story, as it gives Chloe more perspective. Yet I felt like there was also way too much going on to really get into the book. Isobel's story truly interested me, and I wish there was more of her in this book, because I think that her background, and her relationship with Alex, is what could have kept the book going. But those parts seemed few and far between.

There were enjoyable parts to *Ghost House,* but there was also a lot of superfluous information added and it made the story a bit too unbelievable.

—Andrea Modolo

Pretty Deadly, Volume 1: The Shrike by Kelly Sue DeConnick and Emma Ríos

Image Comics, April 30, 2014

What a beautiful comic I have to say. The colours and the ink are absolutely stunning. What really caught my eye was the artfulness of the brushstrokes. They seemed so perfect and so intentionally placed, which for me, really demonstrates the purposefulness and thoughtfulness behind each image.

I love the female characters in this. They're all pretty badass and powerful, each in her own way. It is the women and their secrets and their struggles that drive the story. It's refreshing to see strong female characters who are in control and still manage to keep their clothes on (for the most part). Their truths are slowly revealed throughout each issue and the volume ends on a cliffhanger to assure us that there is more action to come in the next issue.

I did find the story to be a bit rushed. It is such a quick read that the plot doesn't have much time to mature and strengthen. Things that should have taken pages to unravel, were presented in only a few panels. The story itself is so complex that it needs to be given more time to reveal itself to the reader. I do plan on reading it a second time to see what else I can get from it. And plus, who doesn't want to look at beautiful art work for a second time?

This graphic novel is classified as a Western/Fantasy but I wanted to see more of the Fantasy genre throughout. It's definitely there in the images, but I would have loved to see it integrated into the story a little more strongly so it's presence was constant. You do see fantasy brought in with the representation of death and his lair, and you see it in the reaper's ability to enter and interact with Sissy's dreams, but the dream walking is only introduced in the fifth issue. I found this such an intriguing element and it's only mentioned in passing. I wanted to see more.

Overall: beautifully illustrated, compelling storyline, strong characters, but still lacking in the narration. It's a great read and I'll definitely be buying myself a copy of Volume 2 one day. If you're a comic lover, this one's for you.

—Jaaron Collins

Looking for more monsters?
Recommended Reads

Dawson, James. *Say Her Name*. Hot Key Books. 2014

Johnson, Christine (Ed.). *Grim*. Harlequin Teen 2014.

Kagawa, Julie. *The Immortal Rules*. Harlequin Teen. 2012.

Kelly, Nikki. *Lailah*. Feiwel and Friends. 2014.

Kruger, Kat. *The Night Has Teeth*. Fierce Ink Press. 2012.

Livingston, Lesley. *Starling*. HarperTeen. 2012.

McQuein, Josin L. *Arclight*. Green willow Books. 2013.

Morgan, Page. *The Beautiful and the Cursed*. Delacorte Books. 2013.

Ostow, Micol. *Amity*. Egmont. 2014.

Parker, Natalie C. *Beware the Wild*. HarperTeen. 2014.

Roberts, Jeyn. *Dark Inside*. Simon & Schuster Books for Young Readers. 2011.

Shepherd, Megan. *The Madman's Daughter*. HarperTeen. 2012.

Smith, Andrew. *Grasshopper Jungle*. Dutton Juvenile. 2014.

Stiefvater, Maggie. *Sinner*. Scholastic. 2014.

Stolarz, Laurie Faria. *Welcome to the Dark House*. Disney-Hyperion. 2014.

Templeman, McCormick. *The Glass Casket*. Delacorte Press. 2014.

Tucholke, April Genevieve. *Between the Devil and the Deep Blue Sea*. Dial. 2013.

Verday, Jessica. *Of Monsters and Madness*. Egmont. 2014.

Yancey, Rick. *The Monstrumologist*. Simon & Schuster Books for Young Readers. 2009.

Yovanoff, Brenna. *Fiendish*. Razorbill. 2014.

Contributors

S G Larner lives in Brisbane, Australia, and writes short, dark fiction and poetry while juggling three children. Figuratively. You can find her at http://foregoreality.wordpress.com and @StaceySarasvati on twitter.

Amanda Lara lives in Orange County, California. She writes a column for young adults twice a month for *The Fullerton Observer.*

Llanwyre Laish's formative years were filled with the fairy tales and myths of Britain and Ireland. As an adult, she spent nine years sandwiched between gargoyles and rare books, racking up degrees while studying the versions of those tales told in the Middle Ages and the nineteenth century. She now teaches academic writing and writes about roleplaying games.

Kathleen Kelly is a writer from Saskatoon, Saskatchewan. She enjoys regency romance, science fiction and fantasy. When she's not writing, she can be found drinking tea or doing AcroYoga

Aimee Picchi is a freelance journalist and speculative fiction writer who lives in Vermont's biggest city, which is rather small. Her short stories have been published in *The Colored Lens* and *Mirror Dance,* and she's a 2014 graduate of Viable Paradise. She's on Twitter at @aimeepicchi.

Submission Information

We are looking for diverse submissions for each of our upcoming themes. Take the theme and do something unique and unexpected with it. Science fiction, fantasy, paranormal, horror, dystopia, steampunk, cyberpunk, and alternate history welcome.

Requirements:

· 2,000-7,000 words.
· Send to submission.inaccuraterealities@gmail.com with the subject line "Submission. Issue # + Title of Your Story"
· In the body of the e-mail please include your name, story title with word count, byline, address, and any professional publication credits you think relevant.
· Also include the full text of your story in the body of the e-mail in either Times New Roman (12 pt) or Courier (10 pt). Please note that unless we request attachments they will be deleted.
·Submissions are welcome from authors of all ages, as long as the content itself is appropriate for Young Adults.
· Simultaneous submissions are ok. Please let us know, however, if it has been accepted somewhere else.
· You may only submit one story per theme, but you may submit to multiple themes at one time.

Upcoming Issues

Issue 6

Love
Winter 2015

Submissions due: January 15 2015

Issue 7

Hate
Fall 2015

Submissions due: August 15 2015